D1459790

The Subterraneans

WORKS BY JACK KEROUAC
Published by Grove Press

Dr. Sax
Lonesome Traveler
Mexico City Blues
Satori in Paris *and* **Pic**
The Subterraneans

JACK KEROUAC

The Subterraneans

Grove Press
New York

Published simultaneously in Canada
Printed in the United States of America

Library of Congress Catalog Card Number 58-6703
ISBN 978-0-8021-3186-7
eISBN 978-0-8021-9571-5

Grove Press
an imprint of Grove Atlantic
154 West 14th Street
New York, NY 10011

Distributed by Publishers Group West
groveatlantic.com

21 22 23 24 33 32 31 30

The Subterraneans

ONCE I WAS YOUNG and had so much more orientation and could talk with nervous intelligence about everything and with clarity and without as much literary preambling as this; in other words this is the story of an unself-confident man, at the same time of an egomaniac, naturally, facetious won't do—just to start at the beginning and let the truth seep out, that's what I'll do—. It began on a warm summernight—ah, she was sitting on a fender with Julien Alexander who is . . . let me begin with the history of the subterraneans of San Francisco . . .

Julien Alexander is the angel of the subterraneans, the subterraneans is a name invented by Adam Moorad who is a poet and friend of mine who said "They are hip without being slick, they are intelligent without being corny, they are intellectual as hell and know all about Pound without being pretentious or talking too much about it, they are very quiet, they are very Christlike." Julien certainly is Christlike. I was coming down the street with Larry O'Hara old drinking buddy of mine from all the times in San Francisco in my long and nervous and mad careers I've gotten drunk and in fact cadged drinks off friends with such "genial" regularity nobody really cared to notice or announce that I am developing or was developing, in my youth, such bad freeloading habits though of course they did notice but liked me and as Sam said "Everybody comes to you for your gasoline boy, that's some filling station you got there" or

1

say words to that effect—old Larry O'Hara always nice to me,
a crazy Irish young businessman of San Francisco with Balzacian
backroom in his bookstore where they'd smoke tea and talk of
the old days of the great Basie band or the days of the great
Chu Berry—of whom more anon since she got involved with
him too as she had to get involved with everyone because of
knowing me who am nervous and many leveled and not in the
least one-souled—not a piece of my pain has showed yet—or
suffering—Angels, bear with me—I'm not even looking at the
page but straight ahead into the sadglint of my wallroom and
at a Sarah Vaughan Gerry Mulligan Radio KROW show on the
desk in the form of a radio, in other words, they were sitting
on the fender of a car in front of the Black Mask bar on Montgomery Street, Julien Alexander the Christlike unshaved thin
youthful quiet strange almost as you or as Adam might say
apocalyptic angel or saint of the subterraneans, certainly star
(now), and she, Mardou Fox, whose face when first I saw it in
Dante's bar around the corner made me think, "By God, I've
got to get involved with that little woman" and maybe too because she was Negro. Also she had the same face that Rita
Savage a girlhood girlfriend of my sister's had, and of whom
among other things I used to have daydreams of her between
my legs while kneeling on the floor of the toilet, I on the seat,
with her special cool lips and Indian-like hard high soft cheekbones—same face, but dark, sweet, with little eyes honest glittering and intense she Mardou was leaning saying something extremely earnestly to Ross Wallenstein (Julien's friend) leaning
over the table, deep—"I got to get involved with her"—I tried to
shoot her the glad eye the sex eye she never had a notion of
looking up or seeing—I must explain, I'd just come off a ship
in New York, paid off before the trip to Kobe Japan because
of trouble with the steward and my inability to be gracious and
in fact human and like an ordinary guy while performing my
chores as saloon messman (and you must admit now I'm stick-

2

ing to the facts), a thing typical of me, I would treat the first engineer and the other officers with backwards-falling politeness, it finally drove them angry, they wanted me to say something, maybe gruff, in the morning, while setting their coffee down and instead of which silently on crepefeet I rushed to do their bidding and never cracked a smile or if so a sick one, a superior one, all having to do with that loneliness angel riding on my shoulder as I came down warm Montgomery Street that night and saw Mardou on the fender with Julien, remembering, "O there's the girl I gotta get involved with, I wonder if she's going with any of these boys"—dark, you could barely see her in the dim street—her feet in thongs of sandals of such sexuality-looking greatness I wanted to kiss her, them—having no notion of anything though.

The subterraneans were hanging outside the Mask in the warm night, Julien on the fender, Ross Wallenstein standing up, Roger Beloit the great bop tenorman, Walt Fitzpatrick who was the son of a famous director and had grown up in Hollywood in an atmosphere of Greta Garbo parties at dawn and Chaplin falling in the door drunk, several other girls, Harriet the ex-wife of Ross Wallenstein a kind of blonde with soft expressionless features and wearing a simple almost housewife-in-the-kitchen cotton dress but softly bellysweet to look at—as another confession must be made, as many I must make ere time's sup—I am crudely malely sexual and cannot help myself and have lecherous and so on propensities as almost all my male readers no doubt are the same—confession after confession, I am a Canuck, I could not speak English till I was 5 or 6, at 16 I spoke with a halting accent and was a big blue baby in school though varsity basketball later and if not for that no one would have noticed I could cope in any way with the world (underself-confidence) and would have been put in the madhouse for some kind of inadequacy—

But now let me tell Mardou herself (difficult to make a real confession and show what happened when you're such an ego-

3

maniac all you can do is take off on big paragraphs about minor
details about yourself and the big soul details about others
go sitting and waiting around)—in any case, therefore, also
there was Fritz Nicholas the titular leader of the subterraneans,
to whom I said (having met him New Year's Eve in a Nob Hill
swank apartment sitting crosslegged like a peote Indian on a
thick rug wearing a kind of clean white Russian shirt and a
crazy Isadora Duncan girl with long blue hair on his shoulder
smoking pot and talking about Pound and peote) (thin also
Christlike with a faun's look and young and serious and like the
father of the group, as say, suddenly you'd see him in the Black
Mask sitting there with head thrown back thin dark eyes watching everybody as if in sudden slow astonishment and "Here we
are little ones and now what my dears," but also a great dope
man, anything in the form of kicks he would want at any time
and very intense) I said to him, "Do you know this girl, the dark
one?"— "Mardou?"—"That her name? Who she go with?"—
"No one in particular just now, this has been an incestuous group
in its time," a very strange thing he said to me there, as we
walked to his old beat 36 Chevvy with no backseat parked across
from the bar for the purpose of picking up some tea for the
group to get all together, as, I told Larry, "Man, let's get some
tea."—"And what for you want all those people?"—"I want
to dig them as a group," saying this, too, in front of Nicholas
so perhaps he might appreciate my sensitivity being a stranger
to the group and yet immediately, etc., perceiving their value—
facts, facts, sweet philosophy long deserted me with the juices
of other years fled—incestuous—there was another final great
figure in the group who was however now this summer not here
but in Paris, Jack Steen, very interesting Leslie-Howard-like
little guy who walked (as Mardou later imitated for me) like a
Viennese philosopher with soft arms swinging slight side flow
and long slow flowing strides, coming to a stop on corner with
imperious soft pose—he too had had to do with Mardou and as

I learned later most weirdly—but now my first crumb of information concerning this girl I was SEEKING to get involved with as if not enough trouble already or other old romances hadn't taught me that message of pain, keep asking for it, for life—

Out of the bar were pouring interesting people, the night making a great impression on me, some kind of Truman-Capote-haired dark Marlon Brando with a beautiful thin birl or girl in boy slacks with stars in her eyes and hips that seemed so soft when she put her hands in her slacks I could see the change—and dark thin slackpant legs dropping down to little feet, and that face, and with them a guy with another beautiful doll, the guy's name Rob and he's some kind of adventurous Israeli soldier with a British accent whom I suppose you might find in some Riviera bar at 5 A.M. drinking everything in sight alphabetically with a bunch of interesting crazy international-set friends on a spree—Larry O'Hara introducing me to Roger Beloit (I did not believe that this young man with ordinary face in front of me was that great poet I'd revered in my youth, my youth, my youth, that is, 1948, I keep saying my youth)—"This is Roger Beloit?—I'm Bennett Fitzpatrick" (Walt's father) which brought a smile to Roger Beloit's face—Adam Moorad by now having emerged from the night was also there and the night would open—

So we all did go to Larry's and Julien sat on the floor in front of an open newspaper in which was the tea (poor quality L.A. but good enough) and rolled, or "twisted," as Jack Steen, the absent one, had said to me the previous New Year's and that having been my first contact with the subterraneans, he'd asked to roll a stick for me and I'd said really coldly "What for? I roll my own" and immediately the cloud crossed his sensitive little face, etc., and he hated me—and so cut me all the night when he had a chance—but now Julien was on the floor, crosslegged, and himself now twisting for the group and everybody droned the conversations which I certainly won't repeat, except, it was, like, "I'm looking at this book by Percepied— who's Percepied, has he been busted yet?" and such small talk, or, while listening to Stan Kenton talking about the music of tomorrow and we hear a new young tenorman come on, Ricci Comucca, Roger Beloit says, moving back expressive thin purple lips, "This is the music of tomorrow?" and Larry O'Hara telling his usual stock repertoire anecdotes. In the 36 Chevvy on the way, Julien, sitting beside me on the floor, had stuck out his hand and said, "My name's Julien Alexander, I have something, I conquered Egypt," and then Mardou stuck her hand out to Adam Moorad and introduced herself, saying, "Mardou Fox," but didn't think of doing it to me which should have been my first inkling of the prophecy of what was to come, so I had to stick my hand at her and say, "Leo Percepied my name" and shake—ah, you always go for the ones who don't really want you—she really wanted Adam Moorad, she had just been rejected coldly and subterraneanly by Julien—she was interested in thin ascetic strange intellectuals of San Francisco and Berkeley and not in big paranoiac bums of ships and railroads and novels and all that hatefulness which in myself is to myself so evident and so to others too—though and because ten years younger than I seeing none of my virtues which anyway had long been drowned under years of drugtaking and desiring to die, to give up, to give it all up and forget it all, to die in the dark star—it was I stuck out my hand, not she—ah time.

But in eying her little charms I only had the foremost one idea that I had to immerse my lonely being ("A big sad lonely man," is what she said to me one night later, seeing me suddenly in the chair) in the warm bath and salvation of her thighs—the intimacies of younglovers in a bed, high, facing eye to eye, breast to breast naked, organ to organ, knee to shivering goose-pimpled knee, exchanging existential and loveracts for a crack at making it—"making it" the big expression with her, I can see

6

the little out-pushing teeth through the little redlips seeing "making it"—the key to pain—she sat in the corner, by the window, she was being "separated" or "aloof" or "prepared to cut out from this group" for her own reasons.—In the corner I went, not leaning my head on her but on the wall and tried silent communication, then quiet words (as befit party) and North Beach words, "What are you reading?" and for the first time she opened her mouth and spoke to me communicating a full thought and my heart didn't exactly sink but wondered when I heard the cultured funny tones of part Beach, part I. Magnin model, part Berkeley, part Negro highclass, something, a mixture of *langue* and style of talking and use of words I'd never heard before except in certain rare girls of course *white* and so strange even Adam at once noticed and commented with me that night— but definitely the new bop generation way of speaking, you don't say *I*, you say "ahy" or "Oy" and long ways, like oft or erstwhile "effeminate" way of speaking so when you hear it in men at first it has a disagreeable sound and when you hear it in women it's charming but much too strange, and a sound I had already definitely and wonderingly heard in the voice of new bop singers like Jerry Winters especially with Kenton band on the record *Yes Daddy Yes* and maybe in Jeri Southern too— but my heart sank for the Beach has always hated me, cast me out, overlooked me, shat on me, from the beginning in 1943 on in—for look, coming down the street I am some kind of hoodlum and then when they learn I'm not a hoodlum but some kind of crazy saint they don't like it and moreover they're afraid I'll suddenly become a hoodlum anyway and slug them and break things and this I have almost done anyway and in my adolescence did so, as one time I roamed through North Beach with the Stanford basketball team, specifically with Red Kelly whose wife (rightly?) died in Redwood City in 1946, the whole team behind us, the Garetta brothers besides, he pushed a violinist a queer into a doorway and I pushed another one in, he slugged his, I glared at mine, I was 18, I was a nannybeater and fresh as a daisy too—now, seeing this past in the scowl and glare and horror and the beat of my brow-pride they wanted nothing to do with me, and so I of course also knew that Mardou had real genuine distrust and dislike of me as I sat there "trying to (not make IT) but make her"—unhiplike, brash, smiling, the false hysterical "compulsive" smiling they call it—me hot—them cool—and also I had on a very noxious unbeachlike shirt, bought on Broadway in New York when I thought I'd be cutting down the gangplanks in Kobe, a foolish Crosby Hawaiian shirt with designs, which malelike and vain after the original honest humilities of my regular self (really) with the smoking of two drags of tea I felt constrained to open an extra button down and so show my tanned, hairy chest—which must have disgusted her—in any case she didn't look, and spoke little and low—and was intent on Julien who was squatting with his back to her—and she listened and murmured the laughter in the general talk—most of the talk being conducted by O'Hara and loudspeaking Roger Beloit and that intelligent adventurous Rob and I, too silent, listening, digging, but in the tea vanity occasionally throwing in "perfect" (I thought) remarks which were "too perfect" but to Adam Moorad who'd known me all the time clear indication of my awe and listening and respect of the group in fact, and to them this new person throwing in remarks intended to sow his hipness—all horrible, and unredeemable.—Although at first, before the puffs, which were passed around Indian style, I had the definite sensation of being able to come close with Mardou and involved and making her that very first night, that is taking off with her alone if only for coffee but with the puffs which made me pray reverently and in serious secrecy for the return of my pre-puff "sanity" I became extremely unself-confident, overtrying, positive she didn't like me, hating the facts—remembering now the first night I met my Nicki Peters love in 1948 in Adam Moorad's pad in (then) the Fillmore, I was standing unconcerned and beerdrinking in the kitchen as ever (and at home working furiously on a huge novel, mad, cracked, confident, young, talented as never since) when she pointed to my profile shadow on the pale green wall and said, "How beautiful your profile is," which so nonplussed me and (like the tea) made me unself-confident, attentive, attempting to "begin to make her," to act in that way which by her almost hypnotic suggestion now led to the first preliminary probings into pride vs. pride and beauty or beatitude or sensitivity *versus* the stupid neurotic nervousness of the phallic type, forever conscious of his phallus, his tower, of women as wells—the truth of the matter being there, but the man unhinged, unrelaxed, and now it is no longer 1948 but 1953 with cool generations and I five years older, or younger, having to make it (or make the women) with a new style and stow the nervousness—in any case, I gave up consciously trying to make Mardou and settled down to a night of digging the great new perplexing group of subterraneans Adam had discovered and named on the Beach.

But from the first Mardou was indeed self-dependent and independent announcing she wanted no one, nothing to do with anyone, ending (after me) with same—which now in the cold unblessing night I feel in the air, this announcement of hers, and that her little teeth are no longer mine but probably my enemy's lapping at them and giving her the sadistic treatment she probably loves as I had given her none—murders in the air—and that bleak corner where a lamp shines, and winds swirl, a paper, fog, I see the great discouraged face of myself and my so-called love drooping in the lane, no good—as before it had been melancholy droopings in hot chairs, downcast by moons (though tonight's the great night of the harvest moon)—as where then, before, it was the recognition of the need for my return to world-wide love as a great writer should do, like a Luther, a Wagner, now this warm thought of greatness is a big chill in the wind— for greatness dies too—ah and who said I was great —and sup-

9

posing one were a great writer, a secret Shakespeare of the pillow night? or really so—a Baudelaire's poem is not worth his grief—his grief—(It was Mardou finally said to me, "I would have preferred the happy man to the unhappy poems he's left us," which I agree with and I am Baudelaire, and love my brown mistress and I too leaned to her belly and listened to the rumbling underground)—but I should have known from her original announcement of independence to believe in the sincerity of her distaste for involvement, instead hurling on at her as if and because in fact I wanted to be hurt and "lacerate" myself—one more laceration yet and they'll pull the blue sod on, and make my box plop boy—for now death bends big wings over my window, I see it, I hear it, I smell it, I see it in the limp hang of my shirts destined to be not worn, new-old, stylish-out-of-date, neckties snakelike behung I don't even use any more, new blankets for autumn peace beds now writhing rushing cots on the sea of self-murder—loss—hate—paranoia—it was her little face I wanted to enter, and did—

That morning when the party was at its pitch I was in Larry's bedroom again admiring the red light and remembering the night we'd had Micky in there the three of us, Adam and Larry and myself, and had benny and a big sexball amazing to describe in itself—when Larry ran in and said, "Man you gonna make it with her tonight?"—"I'd shore like to—I dunno—."—"Well man find out, ain't much time left, whatsamatter with you, we bring all these people to the house and give em all that tea and now all my beer from the icebox, man we gotta get something out of it, work on it—." "Oh, you like her?"—"I like anybody as far as that goes man—but I *mean*, after all."—Which led me to a short unwillful abortive fresh effort, some look, glance, remark, sitting next to her in corner, I gave up and at dawn she cut out with the others who all went for coffee and I went down there with Adam to see her again (following the group down the stairs five minutes later) and they were there but she wasn't,

10

independently darkly brooding, she'd gone off to her stuffy little place in Heavenly Lane on Telegraph Hill.

So I went home and for several days in sexual phantasies it was she, her dark feet, thongs of sandals, dark eyes, little soft brown face, Rita-Savage-like cheeks and lips, little secretive intimacy and somehow now softly snakelike charm as befits a little thin brown woman disposed to wearing dark clothes, poor beat subterranean clothes. . . .

A few nights later Adam with an evil smile announced he had run into her in a Third Street bus and they'd gone to his place to talk and drink and had a big long talk which Leroy-like culminated in Adam sitting naked reading Chinese poetry and passing the stick and ending up laying in the bed, "And she's very affectionate, God, the way suddenly she wraps her arms around you as if for no other reason but pure sudden affection." —"Are you going to make it? have an affair with her?"—"Well now let me—actually I tell you—she's a whole lot and not a little crazy—she's having therapy, has apparently very seriously flipped only very recently, something to do with Julien, has been having therapy but not showing up, sits or lies down reading or doing nothing but staring at the ceiling all day long in her place, eighteen dollars a month in Heavenly Lane, gets, apparently, some kind of allowance tied up somehow by her doctors or somebody with her inadequacy to work or something—is always talking about it and really too much for my likings—has apparently real hallucinations concerning nuns in the orphanage where she was raised and has seen them and felt actual threat—and also other things, like the sensation of taking junk although she's never had junk but only known junkies." —"Julien?" —"Julien takes junk whenever he can which is not often because he has no money and his ambition like is to be a real junkey— but in any case she had hallucinations of not being properly contact high but actually somehow secretly injected by someone or something, people who follow her down the street, say, and

11

is really crazy—and it's too much for me—and finally being a Negro I don't want to get all involved."—"Is she pretty?"—"Beautiful—but I can't make it."—"But boy I sure dig her looks and everything else."—"Well allright man then you'll make it —go over there, I'll give you the address, or better yet when, I'll invite her here and we'll talk, you can try if you want but although I have a hot feeling sexually and all that for her I really don't want to get any further into her not only for these reasons but finally, the big one, if I'm going to get involved with a girl now I want to be permanent like permanent and serious and long termed and I can't do that with her."—"I'd like a long permanent, et cetera."—"Well we'll see."

He told me of a night she'd be coming for a little snack dinner he'd cook for her so I was there, smoking tea in the red living-room, with a dim red bulb light on, and she came in looking the same but now I was wearing a plain blue silk sports shirt and fancy slacks and I sat back cool to pretend to be cool hoping she would notice this with the result, when the lady entered the parlor I did not rise.

While they ate in the kitchen I pretended to read. I pretended to pay no attention whatever. We went out for a walk the three of us and by now all of us vying to talk like three good friends who want to get in and say everything on their minds, a friendly rivalry—we went to the Red Drum to hear the jazz which that night was Charlie Parker with Honduras Jones on drums and others interesting, probably Roger Beloit too, whom I wanted to see now, and that excitement of softnight San Francisco bop in the air but all in the cool sweet unexerting Beach— so we in fact ran, from Adam's on Telegraph Hill, down the white street under lamps, ran, jumped, showed off, had fun— felt gleeful and something was throbbing and I was pleased that she was able to walk as fast as we were—a nice thin strong little beauty to cut along the street with and so striking everyone

12

turned to see, the strange bearded Adam, dark Mardou in strange slacks, and me, big gleeful hood.

So there we were at the Red Drum, a tableful of beers a few that is and all the gangs cutting in and out, paying a dollar quarter at the door, the little hip-pretending weazel there taking tickets, Paddy Cordavan floating in as prophesied (a big tall blond brakeman type subterranean from Eastern Washington cowboy-looking in jeans coming in to a wild generation party all smoky and mad and I yelled "Paddy Cordavan?" and "Yeah?" and he'd come over)—all sitting together, interesting groups at various tables, Julien, Roxanne (a woman of 25 prophesying the future style of America with short almost crewcut but with curls black snaky hair, snaky walk, pale pale junkey anemic face and we say junkey when once Dostoevsky would have said what? if not ascetic or saintly? but not in the least? but the cold pale booster face of the cold blue girl and wearing a man's white shirt but with the cuffs undone untied at the buttons so I remember her leaning over talking to someone after having slinked across the floor with flowing propelled shoulders, bending to talk with her hand holding a short butt and the neat little flick she was giving it to knock ashes but repeatedly with long long fingernails an inch long and also orient and snake-like)—groups of all kinds, and Ross Wallenstein, the crowd, and up on the stand Bird Parker with solemn eyes who'd been busted fairly recently and had now returned to a kind of bop dead Frisco but had just discovered or been told about the Red Drum, the great new generation gang wailing and gathering there, so here he was on the stand, examining them with his eyes as he blew his now-settled-down-into-regulated-design "crazy" notes—the booming drums, the high ceiling—Adam for my sake dutifully cutting out at about 11 o'clock so he could go to bed and get to work in the morning, after a brief cutout with Paddy and myself for a quick ten-cent beer

13

at roaring Pantera's, where Paddy and I in our first talk and laughter together pulled wrists—now Mardou cut out with me, glee eyed, between sets, for quick beers, but at her insistence at the Mask instead where they were fifteen cents, but she had a few pennies herself and we went there and began earnestly talking and getting hightingled on the beer and now it was the beginning—returning to the Red Drum for sets, to hear Bird, whom I saw distinctly digging Mardou several times also myself directly into my eye looking to search if really I was that great writer I thought myself to be as if he knew my thoughts and ambitions or remembered me from other night clubs and other coasts, other Chicagos—not a challenging look but the king and founder of the bop generation at least the sound of it in digging his audience digging the eyes, the secret eyes him-watching, as he just pursed his lips and let great lungs and immortal fingers work, his eyes separate and interested and humane, the kindest jazz musician there could be while being and therefore naturally the greatest—watching Mardou and me in the infancy of our love and probably wondering why, or knowing it wouldn't last, or seeing who it was would be hurt, as now, obviously, but not quite yet, it was Mardou whose eyes were shining in my direction, though I could not have known and now do not definitely know—except the one fact, on the way home, the session over the beer in the Mask drunk we went home on the Third Street bus sadly through night and throb knock neons and when I suddenly leaned over her to shout something further (in her secret self as later confessed) her heart leapt to smell the "sweetness of my breath" (quote) and suddenly she almost loved me—I not knowing this, as we found the Russian dark sad door of Heavenly Lane a great iron gate rasping on the sidewalk to the pull, the insides of smelling garbage cans sad-leaning together, fish heads, cats, and then the Lane itself, my first view of it (the long history and hugeness of it in my soul, as in 1951 cutting along with my sketchbook on

a wild October evening when I was discovering my own writing
soul at last I saw the subterranean Victor who'd come to Big
Sur once on a motorcycle, was reputed to have gone to Alaska on
same, with little subterranean chick Dorie Kiehl, there he was
in striding Jesus coat heading north to Heavenly Lane to his pad
and I followed him awhile, wondering about Heavenly Lane and
all the long talks I'd been having for years with people like Mac
Jones about the mystery, the silence of the subterraneans, "urban
Thoreaus" Mac called them, as from Alfred Kazin in New
York New School lectures back East commenting on all the
students being interested in Whitman from a sexual revolution
standpoint and in Thoreau from a contemplative mystic and
antimaterialistic as if existentialist or whatever standpoint, the
Pierre-of-Melville goof and wonder of it, the dark little beat
burlap dresses, the stories you'd heard about great tenormen
shooting junk by broken windows and starting at their horns,
or great young poets with bears lying high in Rouault-like saintly
obscurities, Heavenly Lane the famous Heavenly Lane where
they'd all at one time or another the bat subterraneans lived, like
Alfred and his little sickly wife something straight out of Dostoevsky's Petersburg slums you'd think but really the American
lost bearded idealistic—the whole thing in any case), seeing it
for the first time, but with Mardou, the wash hung over the court,
actually the back courtyard of a big 20-family tenement with bay
windows, the wash hung out and in the afternoon the great sym-
phony of Italian mothers, children, fathers BeFinneganing and
yelling from stepladders, smells, cats mewing, Mexicans,
the music from all the radios whether bolero of Mexican or
Italian tenor of spaghetti eaters or loud suddenly turned-up
KPFA symphonies of Vivaldi harpsichord intellectuals perform-
ances boom blam the tremendous sound of it which I then came
to hear all the summer wrapt in the arms of my love—walking in
there now, and going up the narrow musty stairs like in a hovel,
and her door.

Plotting I demanded we dance—previously she'd been hungry so I'd suggested and we'd actually gone and bought egg foo young at Jackson and Kearny and now she heated this (later confession she'd hated it though it's one of my favorite dishes and typical of my later behavior I was already forcing down her throat that which she in subterranean sorrow wanted to endure alone if at all ever), ah.—Dancing, I had put the light out, so, in the dark, dancing, I kissed her—it was giddy, whirling to the dance, the beginning, the usual beginning of lovers kissing standing up in a dark room the room being the woman's the man all designs—ending up later in wild dances she on my lap or thigh as I danced her around bent back for balance and she around my neck her arms that came to warm so much the *me* that then was only hot—

And soon enough I'd learn she had no belief and had had no place to get it from—Negro mother dead for birth of her—unknown Cherokee-halfbreed father a hobo who'd come throwing torn shoes across gray plains of fall in black sombrero and pink scarf squatting by hotdog fires casting Tokay empties into the night "Yaa Calexico!"

Quick to plunge, bite, put the light out, hide my face in shame, make love to her tremendously because of lack of love for a year almost and the need pushing me down—our little agreements in the dark, the really should-not-be-tolds—for it was she who later said "Men are so crazy, they want the essence, the woman is the essence, there it is right in their hands but they rush off erecting big abstract constructions."—"You mean they should just stay home with the essence, that is lie under a tree all day with the woman but Mardou that's an old idea of mine, a lovely idea, I never heard it better expressed and never dreamed."—"Instead they rush off and have big wars and consider women as prizes instead of human beings, well man I may be in the middle of all this shit but I certainly don't want any part of it" (in her sweet cultured hip tones of new genera-

16

tion).—And so having had the essence of her love now I erect
big word constructions and thereby betray it really—telling tales
of every gossip sheet the washline of the world—and hers,
ours, in all the two months of our love (I thought) only once-
washed as she being a lonely subterranean spent mooningdays
and would go to the laundry with them but suddenly it's dank
late afternoon and too late and the sheets are gray, lovely to
me—because soft.—But I cannot in this confession betray the
innermosts, the thighs, what the thighs contain—and yet why
write?—the thighs contain the essence—yet tho there I should
stay and from there I came and'll eventually return, still I have
to rush off and construct construct—for nothing—for Baudelaire poems—

Never did she use the word love, even that first moment after
our wild dance when I carried her still on my lap and hanging
clear to the bed and slowly dumped her, suffered to find her,
which she loved, and being unsexual in her entire life (except
for the first 15-year-old conjugality which for some reason con-
summated her and never since) (O the pain of telling these
secrets which are so necessary to tell, or why write or live) now
"casus in eventu est" but glad to have me losing my mind in the
slight way egomaniacally I might on a few beers.—Lying then
in the dark, soft, tentacled, waiting, till sleep—so in the morning I wake from the scream of beermares and see beside me the
Negro woman with parted lips sleeping, and little bits of white
pillow stuffing in her black hair, feel almost revulsion, realize
what a beast I am for feeling anything near it, grape little sweet-
body naked on the restless sheets of the nightbefore excitement,
the noise in Heavenly Lane sneaking in through the gray window, a gray doomsday in August so I feel like leaving at once
to get "back to my work" the chimera of not the chimera but
the orderly advancing sense of work and duty which I had
worked up and developed at home (in South City) humble as
it is, the comforts there too, the solitude which I wanted and now

17

can't stand.—I got up and began to dress, apologize, she lay like a little mummy in the sheet and cast the serious brown eyes on me, like eyes of Indian watchfulness in a wood, like with the brown lashes suddenly rising with black lashes to reveal sudden fantastic whites of eye with the brown glittering iris center, the seriousness of her face accentuated by the slightly Mongoloid as if of a boxer nose and the cheeks puffed a little from sleep, like the face on a beautiful porphyry mask found long ago and Aztecan.—"But why do you have to rush off so fast, as though almost hysterical or worried?"—"Well I do I have work to do and I have to straighten out—hangover—" and she barely awake, so I sneak out with a few words in fact when she lapses almost into sleep and I don't see her again for a few days—

The adolescent cocksman having made his conquest barely broods at home the loss of the love of the conquered lass, the blacklash lovely—no confession there.—It was on a morning when I slept at Adam's that I saw her again, I was going to rise, do some typing and coffee drinking in the kitchen all day since at that time work, work was my dominant thought, not love—not the pain which impels me to write this even while I don't want to, the pain which won't be eased by the writing of this but heightened, but which will be redeemed, and if only it were a dignified pain and could be placed somewhere other than in this black gutter of shame and loss and noisemaking folly in the night and poor sweat on my brow—Adam rising to go to work, I too, washing, mumbling talk, when the phone rang and it was Mardou, who was going to her therapist, but needed a dime for the bus, living around the corner, "Okay come on over but quick I'm going to work or I'll leave the dime with Leo."—"O is he there?"—"Yes."—In my mind man-thoughts of doing it again and actually looking forward to seeing her suddenly, as if I'd felt she was displeased with our first night (no reason to feel that, previous to the balling she'd lain on my chest eating the egg foo young and dug me with glittering glee eyes) (that

18

tonight my enemy devour?) the thought of which makes me drop my greasy hot brow into a tired hand—O love, fled me—or do telepathies cross sympathetically in the night?—Such cacoëthes him befalls—that the cold lover of lust will earn the warm bleed of spirit—so she came in, 8 A.M., Adam went to work and we were alone and immediately she curled up in my lap, at my invite, in the big stuffed chair and we began to talk, she began to tell her story and I turned on (in the gray day) the dim red bulblight and thus began our true love—

She had to tell me everything—no doubt just the other day she'd already told her whole story to Adam and he'd listened tweaking his beard with a dream in his far-off eye to look attentive and loverman in the bleak eternity, nodding—now with me she was starting all over again but as if (as I thought) to a brother of Adam's a greater lover and bigger, more awful listener and worrier.—There we were in all gray San Francisco of the gray West, you could almost smell rain in the air and far across the land, over the mountains beyond Oakland and out beyond Donner and Truckee was the great desert of Nevada, the wastes leading to Utah, to Colorado, to the cold cold come fall plains where I kept imagining that Cherokee-halfbreed hobo father of hers lying bellydown on a flatcar with the wind furling back his rags and black hat, his brown sad face facing all that land and desolation.—At other moments I imagined him instead working as a picker around Indio and on a hot night he's sitting on a chair on the sidewalk among the joking shirtsleeved men, and he spits and they say, "Hey Hawk Taw, tell us that story agin about the time you stole a taxicab and drove it clear to Manitoba, Canada—d'jever hear him tell that one, Cy?"—I saw the vision of her father, he's standing straight up, proudly, handsome, in the bleak dim red light of America on a corner, nobody knows his name, nobody cares—

Her own little stories about flipping and her minor fugues, cutting across boundaries of the city, and smoking too much

marijuana, which held so much terror for her (in the light of
my own absorptions concerning her father the founder of her
flesh and predecessor terror-ee of her terrors and knower of much
greater flips and madness than she in psychoanalytic-induced
anxieties could ever even summon up to just imagine), formed
just the background for thoughts about the Negroes and Indians
and America in general but with all the overtones of 'new generation' and other historical concerns in which she was now
swirled just like all of us in the Wig and Europe Sadness of us
all, the innocent seriousness with which she told her story and
I'd listened to so often and myself told—wide eyed hugging in
heaven together—hipsters of America in the 1950's sitting in
a dim room—the clash of the streets beyond the window's bare
soft sill.—Concern for her father, because I'd been out there
and sat down on the ground and seen the rail the steel of America covering the ground filled with the bones of old Indians and
Original Americans.—In the cold gray fall in Colorado and Wyo-
ming I'd worked on the land and watched Indian hoboes come
suddenly out of brush by the track and move slowly, hawk
lipped, rill-jawed and wrinkled, into the great shadow of the
light bearing burdenbags and junk talking quietly to one another and so distant from the absorptions of the field hands,
even the Negroes of Cheyenne and Denver streets, the Japs, the
general minority Armenians and Mexicans of the whole West
that to look at a three-or-foursome of Indians crossing a field
and a railroad track is to the senses like something unbelievable
as a dream—you think, "They must be Indians—ain't a soul
looking at 'em—they're goin' that way—nobody notices—doesn't
matter much which way they go—reservation? What have they
got in those brown paper bags?" and only with a great amount of
effort you realize "But they were the inhabitors of this land and
under these huge skies they were the worriers and keeners and
protectors of wives in whole nations gathered around tents—
now the rail that runs over their forefathers' bones leads them

20

onward pointing into infinity, wraiths of humanity treading lightly the surface of the ground so deeply suppurated with the stock of their suffering you only have to dig a foot down to find a baby's hand.—The hotshot passenger train with grashing diesel balls by, browm, browm, the Indians just look up—I see them vanishing like spots—" and sitting in the redbulb room in San Francisco now with sweet Mardou I think, "And this is your father I saw in the gray waste, swallowed by night—from his juices came your lips, your eyes full of suffering and sorrow, and we're not to know his name or name his destiny?"—Her little brown hand is curled in mine, her fingernails are paler than her skin, on her toes too and with her shoes off she has one foot curled in between my thighs for warmth and we talk, we begin our romance on the deeper level of love and histories of respect and shame.—For the greatest key to courage is shame and the blurfaces in the passing train see nothing out on the plain but figures of hoboes rolling out of sight—

"I remember one Sunday, Mike and Rita were over, we had some very strong tea—they said it had volcanic ash in it and it was the strongest they'd ever had."—"Came from L. A.?"—"From Mexico—some guys had driven down in the station wagon and pooled their money, or Tijuana or something, I dunno—Rita was flipping at the time—when we were practically stoned she rose very dramatically and stood there in the middle of the room man saying she felt her nerves burning thru her bones—To see her *flip* right before my eyes—I got nervous and had some kind of idea about Mike, he kept *looking* at me like he wanted to kill me—he has such a funny look anyway—I got out of the house and walked along and didn't know which way to go, my mind kept turning into the several directions that I was thinking of going but my body kept walking straight along Columbus altho I felt the sensation of each of the directions I mentally and emotionally turned into, amazed at all the possible directions you can take with different motives that come in, like

21

it can make you a different *person*—I've often thought of this since childhood, of suppose instead of going up Columbus as I usually did I'd turn into Filbert would something happen that at the time is insignificant enough but would be like enough to influence my whole life in the end?—What's in store for me in the direction I *don't* take?—and all that, so if this had not been such a constant preoccupation that accompanied me in my solitude which I played upon in as many different ways as possible I wouldn't bother now except but seeing the horrible roads this pure *supposing* goes to it took me to *frights*, if I wasn't so damned *persistent*—" and so on deep into the day, a long confusing story only pieces of which and imperfectly I remember, just the mass of the misery in connective form—

Flips in gloomy afternoons in Julien's room and Julien sitting paying no attention to her but staring in the gray moth void stirring only occasionally to close the window or change his knee crossings, eyes round staring in a meditation so long and so mysterious and as I say so Christlike really outwardly lamby it was enough to drive anybody crazy I'd say to live there even one day with Julien or Wallenstein (same type) or Mike Murphy (same type), the subterraneans their gloomy longthoughts enduring.—And the meekened girl waiting in a dark corner, as I remembered so well the time I was at Big Sur and Victor arrived on his literally homemade motorcycle with little Dorie Kiehl, there was a party in Patsy's cottage, beer, candlelight, radio, talk, yet for the first hour the newcomers in their funny ragged clothes and he with that beard and she with those somber serious eyes had sat practically out of sight behind the candlelight shadows so no one could see them and since they said nothing whatever but just (if not listened) meditated, gloomed, endured, finally I even forgot they were there—and later that night they slept in a pup tent in the field in the foggy dew of Pacific Coast Starry Night and with the same humble silence mentioned nothing in the morn—Victor so much in my mind always the central exaggerator of subterranean hip generation tendencies to silence, bohemian mystery, drugs, beard, semi-holiness and, as I came to find later, insurpassable nastiness (like George Sanders in *The Moon and Sixpence*)—so Mardou a healthy girl in her own right and from the windy open ready for love now hid in a musty corner waiting for Julien to speak.—Occasionally in the general "incest" she'd been slyly silently by some consenting arrangement or secret statesmanship shifted or probably just "Hey Ross you take Mardou home tonight I wanta make it with Rita for a change,"—and staying at Ross's for a week, smoking the volcanic ash, she was flipping—(the tense anxiety of improper sex additionally, the premature ejaculations of these anemic *maquereaux* leaving her suspended in tension and wonder).—"I was just an innocent chick when I met them, independent and like well not happy or anything but feeling that I had something to do, I wanted to go to night school, I had several jobs at my trade, binding in Olstad's and small places down around Harrison, the art teacher the old gal at school was saying I could become a great sculptress and I was living with various roommates and buying clothes and making it"—(sucking in her little lip, and that slick 'cuk' in the throat of drawing in breath quickly in sadness and as if with a cold, like in the throats of great drinkers, but she not a drinker but saddener of self) (supreme, dark)—(twining warm arm farther around me) "and he's lying there saying whatsamatter and I can't understand—." She can't understand suddenly what has happened because she's lost her mind, her usual recognition of self, and feels the eerie buzz of mystery, she really does not know who she is and what for and where she is, she looks out the window and this city San Francisco is the big bleak bare stage of some giant joke being perpetrated on her.—"With my back turned I didn't know what Ross was thinking—even doing."—She had no clothes on, she'd risen out of his satisfied sheets to stand in the wash of gray gloomtime thinking what to do, where to go.—And the

23

longer she stood there finger-in-mouth and the more the man said, "What's the matter ba-by"(finally he stopped asking and just let her stand there) the more she could feel the pressure from inside towards bursting and explosion coming on, finally she took a giant step forward with a gulp of fear—everything was clear: danger in the air—it was writ in the shadows, in the gloomy dust behind the drawing table in the corner, in the garbage bags, the gray drain of day seeping down the wall and into the window—in the hollow eyes of people—she ran out of the room.—"What'd he say?"

"Nothing—he didn't move but was just with his head off the pillow when I glanced back in closing the door—I had no clothes on in the alley, it didn't disturb me, I was so intent on this realization of everything I knew I was an innocent child."— "The naked babe, wow."—(And to myself: "My God, this girl, Adam's right she's crazy, like I'd do that, I'd flip like I did on Benzedrine with Honey in 1945 and thought she wanted to use my body for the gang car and the wrecking and flames but I'd certainly never run out into the streets of San Francisco naked tho I might have maybe if I really felt there was need for action, yah") and I looked at her wondering if she, was she telling the truth.—She was in the alley, wondering who she was, night, a thin drizzle of mist, silence of sleeping Frisco, the B-O boats in the bay, the shroud over the bay of great clawmouth fogs, the aureola of funny eerie light being sent up in the middle by the Arcade Hood Droops of the Pillar-templed Alcatraz—her heart thumping in the stillness, the cool dark peace.—Up on a wood fence, waiting—to see if some idea from outside would be sent telling her what to do next and full of import and omen because it had to be right and just once—"One slip in the wrong direction . . . ," her direction kick, should she jump down on one side of fence or other, endless space reaching out in four directions, bleak-hatted men going to work in glistening streets

uncaring of the naked girl hiding in the mist or if they'd been
there and seen her would in a circle stand not touching her just
waiting for the cop-authorities to come and cart her away and
all their uninterested weary eyes flat with blank shame watching
every part of her body—the naked babe.—The longer she hangs
on the fence the less power she'll have finally to really get down
and decide, and upstairs Ross Wallenstein doesn't even move
from that junk-high bed, thinking her in the hall huddling, or
he's gone to sleep anyhow in his own skin and bone.—The rainy
night blooping all over, kissing everywhere men women and
cities in one wash of sad poetry, with honey lines of high-shelved
Angels trumpet-blowing up above the final Orient-shroud Pacific-
huge songs of Paradise, an end to fear below.—She squats on the
fence, the thin drizzle making beads on her brown shoulders,
stars in her hair, her wild now-Indian eyes now staring into
the Black with a little fog emanating from her brown mouth,
the misery like ice crystals on the blankets on the ponies of her
Indian ancestors, the drizzle on the village long ago and the
poorsmoke crawling out of the underground and when a mournful
mother pounded acorns and made mush in hopeless millenniums
—the song of the Asia hunting gang clanking down the final
Alaskan rib of earth to New World Howls (in their eyes and in
Mardou's eyes now the eventual Kingdom of Inca Maya and
vast Azteca shining of gold snake and temples as noble as
Greek, Egypt, the long sleek crack jaws and flattened noses
of Mongolian geniuses creating arts in temple rooms and the
leap of their jaws to speak, till the Cortez Spaniards, the Pizarro
weary old-world sissified pantalooned Dutch bums came smashing
canebrake in savannahs to find shining cities of Indian Eyes
high, landscaped, boulevarded, ritualled, heralded, beflagged in
that selfsame New World Sun the beating heart held up to it)—
her heart beating in the Frisco rain, on the fence, facing last
facts, ready to go run down the land now and go back and fold

25

in again where she was and where was all—consoling herself
with visions of truth—coming down off the fence, on tiptoe
moving ahead, finding a hall, shuddering, sneaking—

"I'd made up my mind, I'd erected some structure, it was like,
but I can't—." Making a new start, starting from flesh in the
rain, "Why should anyone want to harm my little heart, my feet,
my little hands, my skin that I'm wrapt in because God wants
me warm and Inside, my toes—why did God make all this all
so decayable and dieable and harmable and wants to make me
realize and scream—why the wild ground and bodies bare and
breaks—I quaked when the giver creamed, when my father
screamed, my mother dreamed—I started small and ballooned
up and now I'm big and a naked child again and only to cry and
fear. —Ah—Protect yourself, angel of no harm, you who've
never and could never harm and crack another innocent its shell
and thin veiled pain—wrap a robe around you, honey lamb—
protect yourself from rain and wait, till Daddy comes again, and
Mama throws you warm inside her valley of the moon, loom at
the loom of patient time, be happy in the mornings."—Making
a new start, shivering, out of the alley night naked in the skin
and on wood feet to the stained door of some neighbor—knocking
—the woman coming to the door in answer to the frightened
butter knock knuckles, sees the naked browngirl, frightened—
("Here is a woman, a soul in my rain, she looks at me, she is
frightened.")—"Knocking on this perfect stranger's door, sure."
—"Thinking I was just going down the street to Betty's and
back, promised her *meaning* it deeply I'd bring the clothes back
and she did let me in and she got a blanket and wrapped it
around me, then the clothes, and luckily she was alone—an
Italian woman.—And in the alley I'd all come out and *on*, it
was now first clothes, then I'd go to Betty's and get two bucks
—then buy this brooch I'd seen that afternoon at some place
with old seawood in the window, at North Beach, art handicraft
ironwork like, a shoppey, it was the first symbol I was going to

allow myself."—"Sure."—Out of the naked rain to a robe, to innocence shrouding in, then the decoration of God and religious sweetness.—"Like when I had that fist fight with Jack Steen it was in my mind strongly."—"Fist fight with Jack Steen?"—"This was earlier, all the junkies in Ross's room, tying up and shooting with Pusher, you know Pusher, well I took my clothes off there too—it was . . . all . . . part of the same . . . flip . . ."—"But this *clothes*, this *clothes!*" (to myself).—"I stood in the middle of the room flipping and Pusher was plucking at the guitar, just one string, and I went up to him and said, 'Man don't pluck those dirty notes at ME,' and like he just got up without a word and left."—And Jack Steen was furious at her and thought if he hit her and knocked her out with his fists she'd come to her senses so he slugged at her but she was just as strong as he (anemic pale 110 lb. junkey ascetics of America), blam, they fought it out before the weary others.—She'd pulled wrists with Jack, Julien, beat them practically—"Like Julien finally won at wrists but he really furiously had to put me down to do it and hurt me and was really upset" (gleeful little shniffle thru the little outteeth)—so there she'd been fighting it out with Jack Steen and really almost licking him but he was furious and neighbors downstairs called cops who came and had to be explained to— "dancing."—"But that day I'd seen this iron thing, a little brooch with a beautiful dull sheen, to be worn around the neck, you know how nice that would look on my breast."—"On your brown breastbone a dull gold beautiful it would be baby, go on with your amazing story."—"So I immediately needed this brooch in spite of the time, 4 A.M. now, and I had that old coat and shoes and an old dress she gave me, I felt like a streetwalker but I felt no one could tell—I ran to Betty's for the two bucks, woke her up—." She demanded the money, she was coming out of death and money was just the means to get the shiny brooch (the silly means invented by inventors of barter and haggle and styles of who owns who, who owns what—). Then she was running

27

down the street with her $2, going to the store long before it
opened, going for coffee in the cafeteria, sitting at the table
alone, digging the world at last, the gloomy hats, the glistening
sidewalks, the signs announcing baked flounder, the reflections
of rain in paneglass and in pillar mirror, the beauty of the food
counters displaying cold spreads and mountains of crullers and
the steam of the coffee urn.—"How warm the world is, all you
gotta do is get little symbolic coins—they'll let you in for all
the warmth and food you want—you don't have to strip your
skin off and chew your bone in alleyways—these places were
designed to house and comfort bag-and-bone people come to
cry for consolation."—She is sitting there staring at everyone,
the usual sexfiends are afraid to stare back because the vibration
from her eyes is wild, they sense some living danger in the
apocalypse of her tense avid neck and trembling wiry hands.—
"This ain't no woman."—"That crazy Indian she'll kill somebody."—Morning coming, Mardou hurrying gleeful and mind-
swum, absorbed, to the store, to buy the brooch—standing then
in a drugstore at the picture postcard swiveller for a solid two
hours examining each one over and over again minutely because
she only had ten cents left and could only buy two and those
two must be perfect private talismans of the new important
meaning, personal omen emblems—her avid lips slack to see
the little corner meanings of the cable-car shadows, Chinatown,
flower stalls, blue, the clerks wondering: "Two hours she's been
in here, no stockings on, dirty knees, looking at cards, some
Third Street Wino's wife run away, came to the big whiteman
drugstore, never saw a shiny sheen postcard before—." In the
night before they would have seen her up Market Street in
Foster's with her last (again) dime and a glass of milk, crying
into her milk, and men always looking at her, always trying to
make her but now doing nothing because frightened, because
she was like a child—and because: "Why didn't Julien or Jack
Steen or Walt Fitzpatrick give you a place to stay and leave you

28

alone in the corner, or lend you a couple bucks?"—"But they didn't care, they were frightened of me, they *really* didn't want me around, they had like distant objectivity, watching me, asking *nasty* questions—a couple times Julien went into his head-against-mine act like you know 'Whatsamatter, Mardou,' and his routines like that and phony sympathy but he really just was curious to find out why I was flipping—none of them'd ever give me *money*, man."—"Those guys really treated you bad, do you know that?"—"Yeah well they never treat anyone—like they never do anything—you take care of yourself, I'll take care of me."—"Existentialism."—"But American worse cool existentialism and of junkies man, I hung around with them, it was for almost a year by then and I was getting, every time they turned on, a kind of a contact high."—She'd sit with them, they'd go on the nod, in the dead silence she'd wait, sensing the slow snakelike waves of vibration struggling across the room, the eyelids falling, the heads nodding and jerking up again, someone mumbling some disagreeable complaint, "Ma-a-n, I'm drug by that son of a bitch MacDoud with all his routines about how he ain't got enough money for one cap, could he get a half a cap or pay a half—m-a-a-n, I never seen such nowhereness, no s-h-i-t, why don't he just go somewhere and *fade*, um." (That junkey 'um' that follows any out-on-the-limb, and anything one says is out-on-the-limb, statement, *um, he-um*, the self-indulgent baby sob inkept from exploding to the big bawl mawk crackfaced WAAA they feel from the junk regressing their systems to the crib.)—Mardou would be sitting there, and finally high on tea or benny she'd begin to feel like she'd been injected, she'd walk down the street in her flip and actually feel the electric contact with other human beings (in her sensitivity recognizing a fact) but some times she was suspicious because it was someone secretly injecting her and following her down the street who was really responsible for the electric sensation and so independent of any natural law of the universe.—"But you really didn't be-

lieve that—but you did—when I flipped on benny in 1945 I
really believed the girl wanted to use my body to burn it and
put her boy's papers in my pocket so the cops'd think he was
dead—I told her, too."—"Oh what did she do?"—"She said,
'Ooo daddy,' and hugged me and took care of me, Honey was
a wild bitch, she put pancake makeup on my pale—I'd lost
thirty, ten, fifteen pounds—but what happened?"—"I wandered
around with my brooch."—She went into some kind of gift
shop and there was a man in a wheel chair there. (She wandered
into a doorway with cages and green canaries in the glass, she
wanted to touch the beads, watch goldfish, caress the old fat
cat sunning on the floor, stand in the cool green parakeet jungle
of the store high on the green out-of-this-world dart eyes of par-
rots swivelling witless necks to cake and burrow in the mad
feather and to feel that definite communication from them of
birdy terror, the electric spasms of their notice, s q u a w k,
l a w k, l e e k, and the man was extremely strange.)—"Why?"
—"I dunno he was just very strange, he wanted, he talked with
me very clearly and insisting —like intensely looking right at
me and at great length but smiling about the simplest common-
place subjects but we both knew we meant everything else that
we said—you know life—actually it was about the tunnels, the
Stockton Street tunnel and the one they just built on Broadway,
that's the one we talked of the most, but as we talked this a great
electrical current of real understanding passed between us and
I could feel the other levels the infinite number of them of every
intonation in his speech and mine and the world of meaning in
every *word*—I'd never realized before how much is *happening*
all the time, and people *know* it—in their eyes they show it, they
refuse to show it by any other—I stayed a very long time."—
"He must have been a weirdy himself."—"You know, balding,
and queer like, and middleaged, and with that with-neck-cut-off
look or head-on-air," (witless, peaked) "looking all over, I
guess it was his mother the old lady with the Paisley shawl—but

30

my god it would take me all day."—"Wow."—"Out on the street
this beautiful old woman with white hair had come up to me and
saw me, but was asking directions, but liked to talk—." (On
the sunny now lyrical Sunday morning after-rain sidewalk, Easter
in Frisco and all the purple hats out and the lavender coats
parading in the cool gusts and the little girls so tiny with their
just whitened shoes and hopeful coats going slowly in the white
hill streets, churches of old bells busy and downtown around
Market where our tattered holy Negro Joan of Arc wandered
hosannahing in her brown borrowed-from-night skin and heart,
flutters of betting sheets at corner newsstands, watchers at nude
magazines, the flowers on the corner in baskets and the old
Italian in his apron with the newspapers kneeling to water,
and the Chinese father in tight ecstatic suit wheeling the basket-
carriaged baby down Powell with his pink-spot-cheeked wife of
glitter brown eyes in her new bonnet rippling to flap in sun,
there stands Mardou smiling intensely and strangely and the
old eccentric lady not any more conscious of her Negroness than
the kind cripple of the store and because of her out and open
face now, the clear indications of a troubled pure innocent spirit
just risen from a pit in pockmarked earth and by own broken
hands self-pulled to safety and salvation, the two women Mardou
and the old lady in the incredibly sad empty streets of Sunday
after the excitements of Saturday night the great glitter up and
down Market like wash gold dusting and the throb of neons at
O'Farrell and Mason bars with cocktail glass cherrysticks wink-
ing invitation to the open hungering hearts of Saturday and
actually leading only finally to Sunday-morning blue emptiness
just the flutter of a few papers in the gutter and the long white
view to Oakland Sabbath haunted, still—Easter sidewalk of
Frisco as white ships cut in clean blue lines from Sasebo beneath
the Golden Gate's span, the wind that sparkles all the leaves of
Marin here laving the washed glitter of the white kind city, in
the lostpurity clouds high above redbrick track and Embarcadero

pier, the haunted broken hint of song of old Pomos the once only-wanderers of these eleven last American now white-behoused hills, the face of Mardou's father himself now as she raises her face to draw breath to speak in the streets of life materializing huge above America, fading—.) "And like I told her but talked too and when she left she gave me her flower and pinned it on me and called me honey."—"Was she white?"—"Yeah, like, she was very affectionate, very plea-*sant* she seemed to love me—like save me, bring me out—I walked up a hill, up California past Chinatown, someplace I came to a white garage like with a big garage wall and this guy in a swivel chair wanted to know what I wanted, I understood all of my moves as one obligation after another to communicate to whoever not accidentally but by *arrangement* was placed before me, communicate and exchange this news, the vibration and new meaning that I had, about everything happening to everyone all the time everywhere and for them not to worry, nobody as mean as you think or—a colored guy, in the swivel chair, and we had a long confused talk and he was reluctant, I remember, to look in my eyes and really listen to what I was saying."—"But what were you saying?"—"But it's all forgotten now—something as simple and like you'd never expect like those tunnels or the old lady and I hanging-up on streets and directions—but the guy wanted to make it with me, I saw him open his zipper but suddenly he got ashamed, I was turned around and could see it in the glass." (In the white planes of wall garage morning, the phantom man and the girl turned slumped watching in the window that not only reflected the black strange sheepish man secretly staring but the whole office, the chair, the safe, the dank concrete back interiors of garage and dull sheen autos, showing up also unwashed specks of dust from last night's rainsplash and thru the glass the across-the-street immortal balcony of wooden bay-window tenement where suddenly she saw three Negro children in strange attire waving but without yelling at a Negro man four stories below

in overalls and therefore apparently working on Easter, who
waved back as he walked in his own strange direction that bi-
sected suddenly the slow direction being taken by two men, two
hatted, coated ordinary men but carrying one a bottle, the other
a boy of three, stopping now and then to raise the bottle of
Four Star California Sherry and drink as the Frisco A.M. All
Morn Sun wind flapped their tragic topcoats to the side, the
boy bawling, their shadows on the street like shadows of gulls
the color of handmade Italian cigars of deep brown stores at
Columbus and Pacific, now the passage of a fishtail Cadillac in
second gear headed for hilltop houses bay-viewing and some
scented visit of relatives bringing the funny papers, news of
old aunts, candy to some unhappy little boy waiting for Sunday
to end, for the sun to cease pouring thru the French blinds and
paling the potted plants but rather rain and Monday again and
the joy of the woodfence alley where only last night poor Mardou'd almost lost.)—"What'd the colored guy do?"—"He zipped
up again, he wouldn't look at me, he turned away, it was strange
he got ashamed and sat down—it reminded me too when I
was a little girl in Oakland and this man would send us to the
store and give us dimes then he'd open his bathrobe and show
us himself."—"Negro?"—"Yea, in my neighborhood where I
lived—I remember I used to never stay there but my girlfriend
did and I think she even did something with him one time."
—"What'd you do about the guy in the swivel chair?"—"Well,
like I wandered out of there and it was a beautiful day, Easter,
man."—"Gad, Easter where was I?"—"The soft sun, the flowers and here I was going down the street and thinking 'Why did
I allow myself to be bored ever in the past and to compensate
for it got high or drunk or rages or all the tricks people have
because they want anything but serene understanding of just
what there is, which is after all so much, and thinking like
angry social deals,—like angry—kicks—like hasseling over social problems and my race problem, it meant so little and I could

33

feel that great confidence and gold of the morning would slip away eventually and had already started—I could have made my whole life like that morning just on the strength of pure understanding and willingness to live and go along, God it was all the most beautiful thing that ever happened to me in its own way—but it was all sinister."—Ended when she got home to her sisters' house in Oakland and they were furious at her anyway but she told them off and did strange things; she noticed for instance the complicated wiring her eldest sister had done to connect the TV and the radio to the kitchen plug in the ramshackle wood upstairs of their cottage near Seventh and Pine the railroad sooty wood and gargoyle porches like tinder in the sham scrapple slums, the yard nothing but a lot with broken rocks and black wood showing where hoboes Tokay'd last night before moving off across the meatpacking yard to the Mainline rail Tracy-bound thru vast endless impossible Brooklyn-Oakland full of telephone poles and crap and on Saturday nights the wild Negro bars full of whores and the Mexicans Ya-Yaaing in their own saloons and the cop car cruising the long sad avenue riddled with drinkers and the glitter of broken bottles (now in the wood house where she was raised in terror Mardou is squatting against the wall looking at the wires in the half dark and she hears herself speak and doesn't understand why she's saying it except that it must be said, come out, because that day earlier when in her wandering she finally got to wild Third Street among the lines of slugging winos and the bloody drunken Indians with bandages rolling out of alleys and the 10¢ movie house with three features and little children of skid row hotels running on the sidewalk and the pawnshops and the Negro chickenshack jukeboxes and she stood in drowsy sun suddenly listening to bop as if for the first time as it poured out, the intention of the musicians and of the horns and instruments suddenly a mystical unity expressing itself in waves like sinister and again electricity but screaming with palpable aliveness the direct *word* from the vibration, the interchanges of statement, the levels of waving intimation, the smile in sound, the same living insinuation in the way her sister'd arranged those wires wriggled entangled and fraught with intention, innocent looking but actually behind the mask of casual life completely by agreement the mawkish mouth almost sneering snakes of electricity purposely placed she'd been seeing all day and hearing in the music and saw now in the wires), "What are you trying to do actually electrocute me?" so the sisters could see something was really wrong, worse than the youngest of the Fox sisters who was alcoholic and made the wild street and got arrested regularly by the vice squad, some nameless horrible yawning *wrong*, "She smokes dope, she hangs out with all those queer guys with beards in the City."—They called the police and Mardou was taken to the hospital—realizing now, "God, I saw how awful what was really happening and about to happen to me and man I pulled out of it fast, and talked sanely with everyone possible and did everything right, they let me out in 48 hours—the other women were with me, we'd look out the windows and the things they said, they made me see the preciousness of really being *out* of those damn bathrobes and *out* of there and out on the street, the sun, we could see ships, out and FREE man to roam around, how great it really is and how we never appreciate it all glum inside our worries and skins, like *fools* really, or blind spoiled detestable children pouting because . . . they can't get . . . all . . . the . . . candy . . . they want, so I talked to the doctors and told them—." "And you had no place to stay, where was your clothes?"— "Scattered all over—all over the Beach—I had to do something—they let me have this place, some friends of mine, for the summer, I'll have to get out in October."—"In the Lane?" —"Yah."—"Honey let's you and me—would you go to Mexico with me?"—"Yes!"—"If I go to Mexico? that is, if I get the money? altho I do have a hunnerd eighty now and we really actually could go tomorrow and make it—like Indians—I mean

35

cheap and living in the country or in the slums."—"Yes—it
would be so nice to get away now."—"But we could or should
really wait till I get—I'm supposed to get five hundred see—
and—" (and that was when I would have whisked her off into
the bosom of my own life)—she saying "I really don't want
anything more to do with the Beach or any of that gang, man,
that's why—I guess I spoke or agreed too soon, you don't seem
so sure now" (laughing to see me ponder).—"But I'm only
pondering practical problems."—"Nevertheless if I'd have said
'maybe' I bet—oooo that awright," kissing me—the gray day,
the red bulblight, I had never heard such a story from such a
soul except from the great men I had known in my youth, great
heroes of America I'd been buddies with, with whom I'd ad-
ventured and gone to jail and known in raggedy dawns, the
boys beat on curbstones seeing symbols in the saturated gutter,
the Rimbauds and Verlaines of America on Times Square,
kids—no girl had ever moved me with a story of spiritual suffering and so beautifully her soul showing out radiant as an angel
wandering in hell and the hell the selfsame streets I'd roamed in
watching, watching for someone just like her and never dreaming the darkness and the mystery and eventuality of our meeting
in eternity, the hugeness of her face now like the sudden vast
Tiger head on a poster on the back of a woodfence in the smoky
dumpyards Saturday no-school mornings, direct, beautiful, insane, in the rain.—We hugged, we held close—it was like love
now, I was amazed—we made it in the livingroom, gladly, in
chairs, on the bed, slept entwined, satisfied—I would show her
more sexuality—

We woke up late, she'd not gone to her psychoanalyst, she'd
"wasted" her day and when Adam came home and saw us in the
chair again still talking and with the house belittered (coffee cups,
crumbs of cakes I'd bought down on tragic Broadway in the
gray Italianness which was so much like the lost Indianness of

Mardou, tragic America-Frisco with its gray fences, gloomy
sidewalks, doorways of dank, I from the small town and more
recently from sunny Florida East Coast found so frightening).—
"Mardou, you wasted your visit to a therapist, really Leo you
should be ashamed and feel a little responsible, after all—"
"You mean I'm making her lay off her duties . . . I used to do
it with all my girls . . . ah it'll be good for her to miss" (not
knowing her need).—Adam almost joking but also most serious,
"Mardou you must write a letter or call—why don't you call him
now?"—"It's a she doctor, up at City & County."—"Well call
now, here's a dime."—"But I can do it tomorrow, but it's too
late."—"How do you know it's too late—no really, you really
goofed today, and you too Leo you're awfully responsible you
rat." And then a gay supper, two girls coming from outside
(gray crazy outside) to join us, one of them fresh from an over-
land drive from New York with Buddy Pond, the doll an L.A.
hip type with short haircut who immediately pitched into the
dirty kitchen and cooked everybody a delicious supper of black
bean soup (all out of cans) with a few groceries while the other
girl, Adam's, goofed on the phone and Mardou and I sat around
guiltily, darkly in the kitchen drinking stale beer and wondering
if Adam wasn't perhaps really right about what should be done,
how one should pull oneself together, but our stories told, our
love solidified, and something sad come into both our eyes—the
evening proceeding with the gay supper, five of us, the girl with
the short haircut saying later that I was so beautiful she couldn't
look (which later turned out to be an East Coast saying of hers
and Buddy Pond's), "beautiful" so amazing to me, unbelievable,
but must have impressed Mardou, who was anyway during the
supper jealous of the girl's attentions to me and later said so—
my position so airy, secure—and we all went driving in her
foreign convertible car, through now clearing Frisco streets not
gray but opening soft hot reds in the sky between the homes
Mardou and I lying back in the open backseat digging them,

37

the soft shades, commenting, holding hands—they up front like gay young international Paris sets driving through town, the short hair girl driving solemnly, Adam pointing out—going to visit some guy on Russian Hill packing for a New York train and France-bound ship where a few beers, small talk, later troopings on foot with Buddy Pond to some literary friend of Adam's Aylward So-and-So famous for the dialogs in *Current Review*, possessor of a magnificent library, then around the corner to (as I told Aylward) America's greatest wit, Charles Bernard, who had gin, and an old gray queer, and others, and sundry suchlike parties, ending late at night as I made my first foolish mistake in my life and love with Mardou, refusing to go home with all the others at 3 A.M., insisting, tho at Charles' invite, to stay till dawn studying his pornographic (homo male sexual) pictures and listening to Marlene Dietrich records, with Aylward—the others leaving, Mardou tired and too much to drink looking at me meekly and not protesting and seeing how I was, a drunk really, always staying late, freeloading, shouting, foolish—but now loving me so not complaining and on her little bare thonged brown feet padding around the kitchen after me as we mix drinks and even when Bernard claims a pornographic picture has been stolen by her (as she's in the bathroom and he's telling me confidentially, "My dear, I saw her slip it into her pocket, her waist I mean her breast pocket") so that when she comes out of bathroom she senses some of this, the queers around her, the strange drunkard she's with, she complains not— the first of so many indignities piled on her, not on her capacity for suffering but gratuitously on her little female dignities.— Ah I shouldn't have done it, goofed, the long list of parties and drinkings and downcrashings and times I ran out on her, the final shocker being when in a cab together she's insisting I take her home (to sleep) and I can go see Sam alone (in bar) but I jump out of cab, madly ("I never saw anything so maniacal"), and run into another cab and zoom off, leaving her in the night—so when Yuri bangs on her door the following night, and I'm not around, and he's drunk and insists, and jumps on her as he'd been doing, she gave in, she gave in—she gave up—jumping ahead of my story, naming my enemy at once—the pain, why should "the sweet ram of their lunge in love" which has really nothing to do with me in time or space, be like a dagger in my throat?

Waking up, then, from the partying, in Heavenly Lane, again I have the beer nightmare (now a little gin too) and with remorse and again almost and now for no reason revulsion the little white woolly particles from the pillow stuffing in her black almost wiry hair, and her puffed cheeks and little puffed lips, the gloom and dank of Heavenly Lane, and once more "I gotta go home, straighten out"—as tho never I was straight with her, but crooked—never away from my chimerical work room and comfort home, in the alien gray of the world city, in a state of WELL-BEING—. "But why do you always want to rush off so soon?"—"I guess a feeling of well-being at home, that I need, to be straight—like—." "I know baby—but I'm, I miss you in a way I'm jealous that you have a home and a mother who irons your clothes and all that and I haven't—." "When shall I come back, Friday night?"—"But baby it's up to you—to say when."—"But tell me what YOU want."—"But I'm not supposed to."—"But what do you mean s'posed?"—"It's like what they say—about—oh, I dunno" (sighing, turning over in the bed, hiding, burrowing little grape body around, so I go, turn her over, flop on bed, kiss the straight line that runs from her breastbone, a depression there, straight, clear down to her belly-button where it becomes an infinitesimal line and proceeds like as if ruled with pencil on down and then continues just as straight underneath, and need a man get well-being from history and thought as she herself said when he has that, the essence, but still).—The weight of my need to go home, my neurotic fears, hangovers, horrors—"I shouldna—we shouldn't

a gone to Bernard's at all last night—at least we shoulda come
home at three with the others."—"That's what I say baby—but
God" (laughing the shnuffle and making little funny imitation
voice of slurring) "you never do what I ash you t'do."—"Aw
I'm sorry—I love you—do you love me?"—"Man," laughing,
"what do you *mean*"—looking at me warily—"I mean do you
feel affection for me?" even as she's putting brown arm around
my tense big neck.—"Naturally baby."—"But what is the—?"
I want to ask everything, can't, don't, don't know how, what is the
mystery of what I want from you, what is man or woman, love,
what do I mean by love or why do I have to insist and ask and
why do I go and leave you because in your poor wretched little
quarters—"It's the place depresses me—at home I sit in the
yard, under trees, feed my cat."—"Oh man I know it's stuffy
in here—shall I open the blind?"—"No everybody'll see you—
I'll be so glad when the summer's over—when I get that dough
and we go to Mexico."—"Well man, let's like you say go now on
your money that you have now, you say we can really make it."
—"Okay! Okay!" an idea which gains power in my brain as
I take a few swigs of stale beer and consider a dobe hut say
outside Texcoco at five dollars a month and we go to the market
in the early dewy morning she in her sweet brown feet on sandals padding wifelike Ruthlike to follow me, we come, buy
oranges, load up on bread, even wine, local wine, we go home
and cook it up cleanly on our little cooker, we sit together over
coffee writing down our dreams, analyzing them, we make love
on our little bed.—Now Mardou and I are sitting there talking
all this over, daydreaming, a big phantasy—"Well man," with
little teeth outlaughing, "WHEN do we do this—like it's been a
minor flip our whole relationship, all this indecisive clouds and
planning—God."—"Maybe we should wait till I get that royalty
dough—yep! really! it'll be better, cause like that we can get a
typewriter and a three-speed machine and Gerry Mulligan records
and clothes for you and everything we need, like the way it

40

is now we can't do anything."—"Yeah—I dunno" (brooding)
"Man you know I don't have any eyes for that hysterical poverty
deal"—(statements of such sudden pith and hip I get mad and
go home and brood about it for days). "When will you be
back?"—"Well okay, then we'll make it Thursday."—"But if
you really want to make it Friday—don't let me interfere with
your work, baby—maybe you'd like it better to be away longer
times."—"After what you—O I love you—you—." I undress
and stay another three hours, and leave guiltily because the well-
being, the sense of doing what I should has been sacrificed, but
tho sacrificed to healthy love, something is sick in me, lost,
fears—I realize too I have not given Mardou a dime, a loaf of
bread literally, but talk, hugs, kisses, I leave the house and her
unemployment check hasn't come and she has nothing to eat—
"What will you eat?"—"O there's some cans—or I can go to
Adam's maybe—but I don't wanta go there too often—I feel he
resents me now, your friendship has been, I've come between
that certain something you had sort of—." "No you didn't."
—"But it's something else—I don't want to go out, I want to
stay in, see no one"—"Not even me?"—"Not even you, sometimes God I feel that."—"Ah Mardou, I'm all mixed up—I
can't make up my mind—we ought to do something together—
I know what, I'll get a job on the railroad and we'll live together—" this is the great new idea.

(And Charles Bernard, the vastness of the name in the cos-
mogony of my brain, a hero of the Proustian past in the scheme
as I knew it, in the Frisco-alone branch of it, Charles Bernard
who'd been Jane's lover, Jane who'd been shot by Frank, Jane
whom I'd lived with, Marie's best friend, the cold winter rainy
nights when Charles would be crossing the campus saying something witty, the great epics almost here sounding phantom like
and uninteresting if at all believable but the true position and
bigburn importance of not only Charles but a good dozen others
in the light rack of my brain, so Mardou seen in this light, is a

41

little brown body in a gray sheet bed in the slums of Telegraph Hill, huge figure in the history of the night yes but only one among many, the asexuality of the WORK—also the sudden gut joy of beer when the visions of great words in rhythmic order all in one giant archangel book go roaring thru my brain, so I lie in the dark also seeing also hearing the jargon of the future worlds—damajehe eleout ekeke dhdkdk dldoud, ——d, ekeoeu dhdhdkehgyt—better not a more than lther ehe the macmurphy out of that dgardent that which strangely he doth mdodudltkdip —baseeaatra—poor examples because of mechanical needs of typing, of the flow of river sounds, words, dark, leading to the future and attesting to the madness, hollowness, ring and roar of my mind which blessed or unblessed is where trees sing—in a funny wind—well-being believes he'll go to heaven—a word to the wise is enough—"Smart went Crazy," wrote Allen Ginsberg.)

Reason why I didn't go home at 3 A.M.—and example.

2

AT FIRST I HAD DOUBTS, because she was Negro, because she was sloppy (always putting off everything till tomorrow, the dirty room, unwashed sheets—what do I really for Christ's sake care about sheets)—doubts because I knew she'd been seriously insane and could very well be again and one of the first things we did, the first nights, she was going into the bathroom naked in the abandoned hall but the door of her place having a strange squeak it sounded to me (high on tea) like suddenly someone had come up and was standing in the stairwell (like maybe Gonzalez the Mexican sort of bum or hanger-on sort of faggish who kept coming up to her place on the strength of some old friendship she'd had with some Tracy Pachucos to bum little 7 centses from her or two cigarettes and all the time usually when she was at her lowest, sometimes even to take negotiable bottles away), thinking it might be him, or some of the subterraneans, in the hall asking "Is anybody with you?" and she naked, unconcernedly, and like in the alley just stands there saying, "No man, you better come back tomorrow I'm busy I'm not alone," this my tea-revery as I lay there, because the moansqueak of the door had that moan of voices in it, so when she got back from the toilet I told her this (reasoning honesty anyway) (and believing it had been really so, almost, and still believing her actively insane, as on the fence in the alley) but when she heard my confession she said she almost flipped again and was frightened of me and almost got up and ran out—for reasons like this, madness, repeated chances of more madness, I had my "doubts" my male self-contained doubts about her, so reasoned, "I'll just at some time cut out and get me another girl, white, v. nite thighs, etc., and it'll have been a grand affair and I hope I don't hurt her tho."—Ha!—doubts because she cooked sloppily and never cleaned up dishes right away, which as first I didn't like and then came to see she really didn't cook sloppily and did wash the dishes after awhile and at the age of six (she later told me) she was forced to wash dishes for her tyrannical uncle's family and all the time on top of that forced to go out in alley in dark night with garbage pan every night same time where she was convinced the same ghost lurked for her—doubts, doubts—which I have not now in the luxury of time-past.—What a luxury it is to know that now I want her forever to my breast my prize my own woman whom I would defend from all Yuries and anybodies with my fists and anything else, *her* time has come to claim independence, announcing, only yesterday ere I began this tearbook, "I want to be an independent chick with money and cuttin' around."—Yeah, and knowing and screwing everybody, Wanderingfoot," I'm thinking, wandering foot from when we—I'd stood at the bus stop in the cold wind and there were a lot of men there and instead of standing at my side she wandered off in little funny red raincoat and black slacks and went into a shoestore doorway (ALWAYS DO WHAT YOU WANT TO DO AIN'T NOTHIN' I LIKE BETTER THAN A GUY DOIN' WHAT HE WANTS, Leroy always said) so I follow her reluctantly thinking, "She sure has wandering feet to hell with her I'll get another chick" (weakening at this point as reader can tell from tone) but turns out she knew I had only shirt no undershirt and should stand where no wind was, telling me later, the realization that she did not talk naked to anyone in the hall any more than it was wanderingfoot to walk

away to lead me to a warmer waitingplace, that it was no more
than shit, still making no impression on my eager impressionable
ready-to-create construct destroy and die brain—as will be seen
in the great construction of jealousy which I later from a dream
and for reasons of self-laceration recreated. . . . Bear with me
all lover readers who've suffered pangs, bear with me men who
understand that the sea of blackness in a darkeyed woman's
eyes is the lonely sea itself and would you go ask the sea to
explain itself, or ask woman why she crosseth hands on lap
over rose? no—

Doubts, therefore, of, well, Mardou's Negro, naturally not
only my mother but my sister whom I may have to live with
some day and her husband a Southerner and everybody con-
cerned, would be mortified to hell and have nothing to do with
us—like it would preclude completely the possibility of living in
the South, like in that Faulknerian pillar homestead in the Old
Granddad moonlight I'd so long envisioned for myself and there
I am with Doctor Whitley pulling out the panel of my rolltop
desk and we drink to great books and outside the cobwebs
on the pines and old mules clop in soft roads, what would they
say if my mansion lady wife was a black Cherokee, it would cut
my life in half, and all such sundry awful American as if to say
white ambition thoughts or white daydreams.—Doubts galore
too about her body itself, again, and in a funny way really re-
laxing now to her love so surprising myself I couldn't believe
it, I'd seen it in the light one playful night so I—walking
through the Fillmore she insisted we confess everything we'd
been hiding for this first week of our relationship, in order to
see and understand and I gave my first confession, haltingly, "I
thought I saw some kind of black thing I've never seen before,
hanging, like it *scared* me" (laughing)—it must have stabbed
her heart to hear, it seemed to me I felt some kind of shock in
her being at my side as she walked as I divulged this secret
thought—but later in the house with light on we both of us

45

childlike examined said body and looked closely and it wasn't anything pernicious and pizen juices but just bluedark as in all kinds of women and I was really and truly reassured to actually see and make the study with her—but this being a doubt that, confessed, warmed her heart to me and made her see that fundamentally I would never snakelike hide the furthest, not the— but no need to defend, I cannot at all possibly begin to understand who I am or what I am any more, my love for Mardou has completely separated me from any previous phantasies valuable and otherwise—The thing therefore that kept these outburst doubts from holding upper sway in my activity in relating with her was the realization not only that she was sexy and sweet and good for me and I was cutting quite a figure with her on the Beach anyway (and in a sense too now cutting the subterraneans who were becoming progressively deeply colder in their looks towards me in Dante's and on street from natural reasons that I had taken over their play doll and one of their really if not the most brilliant gals in their orbit)—Adam also saying, "You go well together and it's good for you," he being at the time and still my artistic and paternal manager—not only this, but, hard to confess, to show how abstract the life in the city of the Talking Class to which we all belong, the Talking Class trying to rationalize itself I suppose out of a really base almost lecherous lustful materialism—it was the reading, the sudden illuminated glad wondrous discovery of Wilhelm Reich, his book *The Function of the Orgasm*, clarity as I had not seen in a long time, not since perhaps the clarity of personal modern grief of Céline, or, say, the clarity of Carmody's mind in 1945 when I first sat at his feet, the clarity of the poesy of Wolfe (at 19 it was clarity for me), the clarity here tho was scientific, Germanic, beautiful, true—something I'd always known and closely indeed connected to my 1948 sudden notion that the only thing that really mattered was love, the lovers going to and fro beneath the boughs in the Forest of Arden of the World, here magnified

46

and at the same time microcosmed and pointed in and maled
into: orgasm—the reflexes of the orgasm—you can't be healthy
without normal sex love and orgasm—I won't go into Reich's
theory since it is available in his own book—but at the same
time Mardou kept saying "O don't pull that Reich on me in bed,
I read his damn book, I don't want our relationship all pointed
out and f . . . . d up with what HE said," (and I'd noticed that
all the subterraneans and practically all intellectuals I have
known have really in the strangest way always put down Reich
if not at first, after awhile)—besides which, Mardou did not
gain orgasm from normal copulation and only after awhile from
stimulation as applied by myself (an old trick that I had learned
with a previous frigid wife) so it wasn't so great of me to make
her come but as she finally only yesterday said "You're doing
this just to give me the pleasure of coming, you're so kind,"
which was a statement suddenly hard for either one of us to
believe and came on the heels of her "I think we ought to
break up, we never do anything together, and I want to be in-
dep—" and so doubts I had of Mardou, that I the great Finn
Macpossipy should take her for my long love wife here there or
anywhere and with all the objections my family, especially my
really but sweetly but nevertheless really tyrannical (because
of my subjective view of her and her influence) mother's sway
over me—sway or whatever.—"Leo, I don't think it's good for
you to live with your mother always," Mardou, a statement that
in my early confidence only made me think, "Well naturally
she, she's just jealous, and has no folks herself, and is one of
those modern psychoanalyzed people who hate mothers anyway"
—out loud saying, "I really do really love her and love you too
and don't you see how hard I try to spend my time, divide my
time between the two of you—over there it's my writing work,
my well-being and when she comes home from work at night,
tired, from the store, mind you, I feel very good making her
supper, having the supper and a martini ready when she walks

in so by 8 o'clock the dishes are all cleared, see, and she has
more time to look at her television—which I worked on the
railroad six months to buy her, see."—Well you've done a lot
of things for her," and Adam Moorad (whom my mother considered mad and evil) too had once said "You've really done
a lot for her, Leo, forget her for a while, you've got your own
life to live," which is exactly what my mother always was telling
me in the dark of the South San Francisco night when we re-
laxed with Tom Collinses under the moon and neighbors would
join us, "You have your own life to live, I won't interfere, Ti
Leo, with anything you want to do, you decide, of course it will
be all right with me," me sitting there goopy realizing it's all
myself, a big subjective phantasy that my mother really needs
me and would die if I weren't around, and nevertheless having
a bellyful of other rationalizations allowing me to rush off two
or three times a year on gigantic voyages to Mexico or New
York or Panama Canal on ships—A million doubts of Mardou,
now dispelled, now (and even without the help of Reich who
shows how life is simply the man entering the woman and the
rubbing of the two in soft—that essence, that dingdong essence—something making me now almost so mad as to shout,
I GOT MY OWN LITTLE BANGTAIL ESSENCE AND THAT
ESSENCE IS MIND RECOGNITION—) now no more doubts.
Even, a thousand times, I without even remembering later asked
her if she'd really stolen the pornographic picture from Bernard
and the last time finally she fired "But I've told you and told
you, about eight times in all, I did not take that picture and
I told you too a thousand times I don't even didn't even have
any pockets whatever in that particular suit I was wearing that
night—no pockets at all," yet it never making an impression
(in feverish folly brain me) that it was Bernard now who was
really crazy, Bernard had gotten older and developed some personal sad foible, accusing others of stealing, solemnly—"Leo
don't you see and you keep asking it"—this being the last deepest

final doubt I wanted about Mardou that she was really a thief of
some sort and therefore was out to steal my heart, my white man
heart, a Negress sneaking in the world sneaking the holy white
men for sacrificial rituals later when they'll be roasted and
roiled (remembering the Tennessee Williams story about the
Negro Turkish bath attendant and the little white fag) because,
not only Ross Wallenstein had called me to my face a fag—
"Man what are you, a fag? you talk you just like a fag," saying
this after I'd said to him in what I hoped were cultured tones,
"You're on goofballs tonight? you ought to try three sometimes,
they'll really knock you out and have a few beers too, but don't
take four, just three," it insulting him completely since he is
the veteran hipster of the Beach and for anyone especially a
brash newcomer stealing Mardou from his group and at the
same time hoodlum-looking with a reputation as a great writer,
which he didn't see, from only published book—the whole mess
of it, Mardou becoming the big buck nigger Turkish bath attendant, and I the little fag who's broken to bits in the love
affair and carried to the bay in a burlap bag, there to be distributed piece by piece and broken bone by bone to the fish if
there are still fish in that sad water)—so she'd thieve my soul
and eat it—so told me a thousand times, "I did not steal that
picture and I'm sure Aylward whatshisname didn't and you
didn't it's just Bernard, he's got some kind of fetish there"—
But it never impressed and stayed till the last, only the other
night, time—that deepest doubt about her arising too from the
time, (which she'd told me about) she was living in Jack Steen's
pad in a crazy loft down on Commercial Street near the sea-
men's union halls, in the glooms, had sat in front of his suit-
case an hour thinking whether she ought to look in it to see
what he had there, then Jack came home and rummaged in it
and thought or saw something was missing and said, sinister,
sullen, "Have you been going thru my bag?" and she almost
leaped up and cried YES because she HAD—"Man I had, in

Mind, been going thru that bag all day and suddenly he was looking at me, with that look—I almost flipped"—that story also not impressing into my rigid paranoia-ridden brain, so for two months I went around thinking she'd told me, "Yes, I did go thru his bag but of course took nothing," but so I saw she'd lied to Jack Steen in reality—but in reality now, the facts, she had only thought to do so, and so on—my doubts all of them hastily ably assisted by a driving paranoia, which is really my confession—doubts, then, all gone.

For now I want Mardou—she just told me that six months ago a disease took root deeply in her soul, and forever now—doesn't this make her more beautiful?—But I want Mardou—because I see her standing, with her black velvet slacks, handsapockets, thin, slouched, cig hanging from lips, the smoke itself curling up, her little black back hairs of short haircut combed down fine and sleek, her lipstick, pale brown skin, dark eyes, the way shadows play on her high cheekbones, the nose, the little soft shape of chin to neck, the little Adam's apple, so hip, so cool, so beautiful, so modern, so new, so unattainable to sad bagpants me in my shack in the middle of the woods—I want her because of the way she imitated Jack Steen that time on the street and it amazed me so much but Adam Moorad was solemn watching the imitation as if perhaps engrossed in the thing itself, or just skeptical, but she disengaged herself from the two men she was walking with and went ahead of them showing the walk (among crowds) the soft swing of arms, the long cool strides, the stop on the corner to hang and softly face up to birds with like as I say Viennese philosopher—but to see her do it, and to a T, (as I'd seen his walk indeed across the park), the fact of her—I love her but this song is . . . broken—but in French now . . . in French I can sing her on and on. . . .

Our little pleasures at home at night, she eats an orange, she makes a lot of noise sucking it—

When I laugh she looks at me with little round black eyes that hide themselves in her lids because she laughs hard (contorting all her face, showing the little teeth, making lights everywhere) (the first time I saw her, at Larry O'Hara's, in the corner, I remember, I'd put my face close to hers to talk about books, she'd turned her face to me close, it was an ocean of melting things and drowning, I could have swimmed in it, I was afraid of all that richness and looked away)—

With her rose bandana she always puts on for the pleasures of the bed, like a gypsy, rose, and then later the purple one, and the little hairs falling black from the phosphorescent purple in her brow as brown as wood—

Her little eyes moving like cats —

We play Gerry Mulligan loud when he arrives in the night, she listens and chews her fingernails, her head moves slowly side to side like a nun in profound prayer—

When she smokes she raises the cigarette to her mouth and slits her eyes—

She reads till gray dawn, head on one arm, *Don Quixote*, Proust, anything—

We lie down, look at each other seriously saying nothing, head to head on the pillow—

Sometimes when she speaks and I have my head under hers on the pillow and I see her jaw the dimple the woman in her neck, I see her deeply, richly, the neck, the deep chin, I know she's one of the most *enwomaned* women I've seen, a brunette of eternity incomprehensibly beautiful and for always sad, profound, calm—

When I catch her in the house, small, squeeze her, she yells out, tickles me furiously, I laugh, she laughs, her eyes shine, she punches me, she wants to beat me with a switch, she says she likes me—

I'm hiding with her in the secret house of the night—

Dawn finds us mystical in our shrouds, heart to heart—

'My sister!' I'd thought suddenly the first time I saw her—

The light is out.

Daydreams of she and I bowing at big fellaheen cocktail parties somehow with glittering Parises in the horizon and in the forefront—she's crossing the long planks of my floor with a smile.

Always putting her to a test, which goes with "doubts"— doubts indeed—and I would like to accuse myself of bastardliness—such tests—briefly I can name two, the night Arial Lavalina the famous young writer suddenly was standing in the Mask and I was sitting with Carmody also now famous writer in a way who'd just arrived from North Africa, Mardou around the corner in Dante's cutting back and forth as was our wont all around, from bar to bar, and sometimes she'd cut unescorted there to see the Juliens and others—I saw Lavalina and called his name and he came over.—When Mardou came to get me to go home I wouldn't go, I kept insisting it was an important literary moment, the meeting of those two (Carmody having plotted with me a year earlier in dark Mexico when we'd lived poor and beat and he's a junkey, "Write a letter to Ralph Lowry find out how I can get to meet this here good-looking Arial Lavalina, man, look at that picture on the back of *Recognition of Rome,* ain't that something?" my sympathies with him in the matter being personal and again like Bernard also queer he was connected with the legend of the bigbrain of myself which was my WORK, that all consuming work, so wrote the letter and all that) but now suddenly (after of course no reply from the Ischia and otherwise grapevines and certainly just as well for me at least) he was standing there and I recognized him from the night I'd met him at the Met ballet when in New York in tux I'd cut out with tuxed editor to see glitter nightworld New York of letters and wit, and Leon Danillian, so I yelled "Arial Lavalina! come here!" which he did.—When Mardou came I said whispering gleefully "This is Arial Lavalina ain't that mad!"—"Yeh man but I want to go home."—And in those days her love meaning no more to me

than that I had a nice convenient dog chasing after me (much
like in my real secretive Mexican vision of her following me
down dark dobe streets of slums of Mexico City not walking
with me but following, like Indian woman) I just goofed and
said "But wait, you go home and wait for me, I want to dig
Arial and then I'll be home."—"But baby you said that the
other night and you were two hours late and you don't know
what pain it caused me to wait." (Pain!)—"I know but look,"
and so I took her around the block to persuade her, and drunk
as usual at one point to prove something I stood on my head in
the pavement of Montgomery or Clay Street and some hoodlums
passed by, saw this, saying "That's right"—finally (she laughing)
depositing her in a cab, to get home, wait for me—going back
to Lavalina and Carmody whom gleefully and now alone back
in my big world night adolescent literary vision of the world,
with nose pressed to window glass, "Will you look at that,
Carmody and Lavalina, the great Arial Lavalina tho not a great
great writer like me nevertheless so famous and glamorous etc.
together in the Mask and I arranged it and everything ties together, the myth of the rainy night, Master Mad, Raw Road,
going back to 1949 and 1950 and all things grand great the
Mask of old history crusts"—(this my feeling and I go in) and
sit with them and drink further—repairing the three of us to 13
Pater a lesbian joint down Columbus, Carmody, high, leaving us
to go enjoy it, and we sitting in there, further beers, the horror
the unspeakable horror of myself suddenly finding in myself a
kind of perhaps William Blake or Crazy Jane or really Chris-
topher Smart alcoholic humility grabbing and kissing Arial's
hand and exclaiming "Oh Arial you dear—you are going to be
—you are so famous—you wrote so well— I remember you—
what—" whatever and now unrememberable and drunkenness,
and there he is a well-known and perfectly obvious homosexual
of the first water, my roaring brain— we go to his suite in some
hotel—I wake up in the morning on the couch, filled with the

53

first horrible recognition, "I didn't go back to Mardou's at all"
so in the cab he gives me—I ask for fifty cents but he gives me
a dollar saying "You owe me a dollar" and I rush out and walk
fast in the hot sun face all broken from drinking and chagrin
to her place down in Heavenly Lane arriving just as she's dress-
ing up to go to the therapist.—Ah sad Mardou with little dark
eyes looking with pain and had waited all night in a dark bed
and the drunken man leering in and I rushed down in fact at
once to get two cans of beer to straighten up ("To curb the
fearful hounds of hair" Old Bull Balloon would say), so as she
abluted to go out I yelled and cavorted—went to sleep, to wait
for her return, which was in the late afternoon, waking to hear
the cry of pure children in the alleyways down there—the horror
the horror, and deciding, "I'll write a letter at once to Lavalina,"
enclosing a dollar and apologizing for getting so drunk and acting in such a way as to mislead him—Mardou returning, no
complaints, only a few a little later, and the days rolling and
passing and still she forgives me enough or is humble enough
in the wake of my crashing star in fact to write me, a few nights
later, this letter:

DEAR BABY,

*Isn't it good to know winter
is coming—*

as we'd been complaining so much about heat and now the heat
was ended, a coolness came into the air, you could feel it in the
draining gray airshaft of Heavenly Lane and in the look of the
sky and nights with a greater wavy glitter in streetlights—

*—and that life will be a little more quiet—and you will
be home writing and eating well and we will be spending pleasant nights wrapped round one another—and*

54

you are home now, rested and eating well because you should not become too sad—

written after, one night, in the Mask with her and newly arrived and future enemy Yuri erstwhile close lil brother I'd suddenly said "I feel impossibly sad and like I'll die, what can we do?" and Yuri'd suggested "Call Sam," which, in my sadness, I did, and so earnestly, as otherwise he'd pay no attention being a newspaper man and new father and no time to goof, but so earnestly he accepted us, the three, to come at once, from the Mask, to his apartment on Russian Hill, where we went, I getting drunker than ever, Sam as ever punching me and saying "The trouble with you, Percepied," and, "You've got rotten bags in the bottom of your store," and, "You Canucks are really all alike and I don't even believe you'll admit it when you die"—Mardou watching amused, drinking a little, Sam finally, as always falling over drunk, but not really, drunk-desiring, over a little lowtable covered a foot high with ashtrays piled three inches high and drinks and doodads, crash, his wife, with baby just from crib, sighing—Yuri, who didn't drink but only watched bead-eyed, after having said to me the first day of his arrival, "You know Percepied I really like you now, I really feel like communicating with you now," which I should have suspected, in him, as constituting a new kind of sinister interest in the innocence of my activities, that being by the name of, Mardou—

—because you should not become too sad

was only sweet comment heartbreakable Mardou made about that disastrous awful night—similar to example 2, one following the one with Lavalina, the night of the beautiful faun boy who'd been in bed with Micky two years before at a great depraved wildparty I'd myself arranged in days when living with Micky the great doll of the roaring legend night, seeing him in the Mask, and being with Frank Carmody and everybody, tugging at his shirt, insisting he follow us to other bars, follow us around, Mardou finally in the blur and roar of the night yelling at me "It's him or me goddamit," but not really serious (herself usually not a drinker because a subterranean but in her affair with Percepied a big drinker now)—she left, I heard her say "We're through" but never for a moment believed it and it was not so, she came back later, I saw her again, we swayed together, once more I'd been a bad boy and again ludicrously like a fag, this distressing me again in waking in gray Heavenly Lane in the morning beer roared.—This is the confession of a man who can't drink.—And so her letter saying:

> *because you should not become too sad—and I feel better when you are well—*

forgiving, forgetting all this sad folly when all she wants to do, "I don't want to go out drinking and getting drunk with all your friends and keep going to Dante's and see all those Juliens and everybody again, I want us to stay quiet at home, listen to KPFA and read or something, or go to a show, baby I like shows, movies on Market Street, I really do."—"But I hate movies, life's more interesting!" (another putdown)—her sweet letter continuing:

> *I am full of strange feelings, reliving and refashioning many old things*

—when she was 14 or 13 maybe she'd play hookey from school in Oakland and take the ferry to Market Street and spend all day in one movie, wandering around having hallucinated phantasies, looking at all the eyes, a little Negro girl roaming the shuffle restless street of winos, hoodlums, sams, cops, paper peddlers, the mad mixup there the crowd eying looking everywhere the sexfiend crowd and all of it in the gray rain of hookey days—poor Mardou—"I'd get sexual phantasies the strangest

kind, not with like sex acts with people but strange situations
that I'd spend all day working out as I walked, and my orgasms
the few I had only came, because I never masturbated or even
knew how, when I dreamed that my father or somebody was
leaving me, running away from me, I'd wake up with a funny
convulsion and wetness in myself, in my thighs, and on Market
Street the same way but different and anxiety dreams woven out
of the movies I saw."—Me thinking *O grayscreen gangster cocktail rainyday roaring gunshot spectral immortality B movie tire
pile black-in-the-mist Wildamerica but it's a crazy world!*—
"Honey" (out loud) "wished I could have seen you walking
around Market like that—I bet I DID see you—I bet I did—
you were thirteen and I was twenty-two—1944, yeah I bet I saw
you, I was a seaman, I was always there, I knew the gangs
around the bars—" So in her letter saying:

> *reliving and refashioning many old things*

probably reliving those days and phantasies, and earlier cruder
horrors of home in Oakland where her aunt hysterically beat
her or hysterically tried and her sisters (tho occasional little-
sister tenderness like dutiful kisses before bed and writing on
one another's backs) giving her a bad time, and she roaming
the street late, deep in broodthoughts and men trying to make
her, the dark men of dark colored-district doors—so going on,

> *and feeling the cold and the quietude even in the
> midst of my forebodings and fears—which clear nights
> soothe and make more sharp and real—tangible and
> easier to cope with*

—said indeed with a nice rhythm, too, so I remember admiring her intelligence even then—but at the same time darkening
at home there at my desk of well-being and thinking, "But cope
that old psychoanalytic cope, she talks like all of em, the city

decadent intellectual dead-ended in cause-and-effect analysis and solution of so-called problems instead of the great JOY of being and will and fearlessness—rupture's their rapture—that's her trouble, she's just like Adam, like Julien, the lot, afraid of madness, the fear of madness haunts her—not Me Not Me by God"—

But why am I writing to say these things to you. But all feelings are real and you probably discern or feel too what I am saying and why I need to write it—

—a sentiment of mystery and charm—but, as I told her often, not enough detail, the details are the life of it, I insist, say everything on your mind, don't hold it back, don't analyze or anything as you go along, say it out, "That's" (I now say in reading letter) "a typical example—but no mind, she's just a girl—humph"—

My image of you now is strange

—I see the bough of that statement, it waves on the tree—

I feel a distance from you which you might feel too which gives me a picture of you that is warm and friendly

and then inserts, in smaller writing,

(and loving)

to obviate my feeling depressed probably over seeing in a letter from lover only word "friendly"—but that whole complicated phrase further complicated by the fact it is presented in originally written form under the marks and additions of a rewrite, which is not as interesting to me, naturally—the rewrite being

I feel a distance from you which you might feel too

58

*with pictures of you that are warm and friendly (and
loving)
—and because of the anxieties we are experiencing
but never speak of really, and are similar too—*

a piece of communication making me suddenly by some majesty
of her pen feel sorry for myself, seeing myself like her lost in the
suffering ignorant sea of human life feeling distant from she
who should be closest and not knowing (no not under the sun)
why the distance instead is the feeling, the both of us entwined
and lost in that, as under the sea—

I am going to sleep to dream, to wake

—hints of our business of writing down dreams or telling
dreams on waking, all the strange dreams indeed and (later
will show) the further brain communicating we did, telepathiz-
ing images together with eyes closed, where it will be shown,
all thoughts meet in the crystal chandelier of eternity—Jim—
yet I also like the rhythm of *to dream, to wake,* and flatter myself I have a rhythmic girl in any case, at my metaphysical
homedesk—

*You have a very beautiful face and I like to see it as
I do now—*

—echoes of that New York girl's statement and now coming
from humble meek Mardou not so unbelievable and I actually
begin to preen and believe in this (O humble paper of letters,
O the time I sat on a log near Idlewild airport in New York and
watched the helicopter flying in with the mail and as I looked
I saw the smile of all the angels of earth who'd written the
letters which were packed in its hold, the smiles of them, specifically of my mother, bending over sweet paper and pen to communicate by mail with her daughter, the angelical smile like

59

the smiles of workingwomen in factories, the world-wide bliss of it and the courage and beauty of it, recognition of which facts I shouldn't even deserve, treating Mardou as I have done) (O forgive me angels of the heaven and of the earth—even Ross Wallenstein will go to heaven)—

> *Forgive the conjunctions and double infinitives and the not said*

—again I'm impressed and I think, she too there, for the first time self-conscious of writing to an author—

> *I don't know really what I wanted to say but want you to have a few words from me this Wednesday morning*

and the mail only carried it in much later, after I saw her, the letter losing therefore its hopeful impactedness

> *We are like two animals escaping to dark warm holes and live our pains alone*

—at this time my dumb phantasy of the two of us (after all the drunks making me drunksick city sick) was, a shack in the middle of the Mississippi woods, Mardou with me, damn the lynchers, the not-likings, so I wrote back: "I hope you meant by that line (*animals to dark warm holes*) you'll turn out to be the woman who can really live with me in profound solitude of woods finally and at same time make the glittering Parises (there it is) and grow old with me in my cottage of peace" (suddenly seeing myself as William Blake with the meek wife in the middle of London early dewy morning, Crabbe Robinson is coming with some more etching work but Blake is lost in the vision of the Lamb at breakfast leavings table).—Ah regrettable Mardou, and never a thought of that thing beats in your brow, that I should kiss, the pain of your own pride, enough

19th-century romantic general talk—the details are the life of
it—(a man may act stupid and top tippity and bigtime 19th-
century boss type dominant with a woman but it won't help him
when the chips are down—the loss lass'll make it back, it's
hidden in her eyes, her future triumph and strength—on his
lips we hear nothing but "of course love").—Her closing words a
beautiful pastichepattisee, or pie, of—

> *Write to me   anything   Please Stay Well Your Freind*
> [misspelled]   *And my love   And Oh*   [over some
> kind of hiddenforever erasures]   [and many X's for of
> course kisses]   *And Love for You*   MARDOU
> [underlined]

and weirdest, most strange, central of all—ringed by itself, the
word, PLEASE—her lastplea neither one of us knowing—Answering this letter myself with a dull boloney bullshit rising out of
my anger with the incident of the pushcart.

(And tonight this letter is my last hope.)

The incident of the pushcart began, again as usual, in the
Mask and Dante's, drinking, I'd come in to see Mardou from
my work, we were in a drinking mood, for some reason suddenly I wanted to drink red Burgundy wine which I'd tasted
with Frank and Adam and Yuri the Sunday before—another,
and first, worthy of mention incident, being—but that's the
crux of it all—THE DREAM. Oh the bloody dream! In which
there was a pushcart, and everything else prophesied. This too
after a night of severe drinking, the night of the redshirt faun
boy—where everybody afterward of course said "You made
a fool of yourself, Leo, you're making yourself a reputation
on the Beach as a big fag tugging at the shirts of well-known
punks."—"But I only wanted him for you to dig."—"Nevertheless" (Adam) "*really*."—And Frank: "You really makin a

horrible reputation."—Me: "I don't care, you remember 1948 when Sylvester Strauss that fag composer got sore at me because I wouldn't go to bed with him because he'd read my novel and submitted it, yelled at me 'I know all about you and your awful reputation.'—'What?'—'You and that there Sam Vedder go around the Beach picking up sailors and giving them dope and he makes them only so he can bite, I've heard about you.'— 'Where did you hear this fantastic tale?'—you know that story, Frank."—"I should imagine" (Frank laughing) "what with all the things you do right there in the Mask, drunk, in front of everybody, if I didn't know you I'd swear you were the craziest piece of rough trade that ever walked" (a typical Carmodian pithy statement) and Adam "Really that's true."—After the night of the redshirt boy, drunk, I'd slept with Mardou and had the worst nightmare of all, which was, everybody, the whole world was around our bed, we lay there and everything was happening. Dead Jane was there, had a big bottle of Tokay wine hidden in Mardou's dresser for me and got it out and poured me a big slug and spilled a lot out of the waterglass on the bed (a symbol of even further drinking, more wine, to come)—and Frank with her—and Adam, who went out the door to the dark tragic Italian pushcart Telegraph Hill street, going down the rickety wooden Shatov stairs where the subterraneans were "digging an old Jewish patriarch just arrived from Russia" who is holding some ritual by the barrels of the fish head cats (the fish heads, in the height of the hot days Mardou had a fish head for our crazy little visiting cat who was almost human in his insistence to be loved his scrolling of neck and purring to be against you, for him she had a fish head which smelled so horrible in the almost airless night I threw part of it out in the barrel downstairs after first throwing a piece of slimy gut unbeknownst I'd put my hands against in the dark icebox where was a small piece of ice I wanted to chill my sauterne with, smack against a great soft mass, the guts or mouth of a fish, this being left in the icebox after disposal of fish I threw it out, the piece draped over fire escape and was there all hotnight and so in the morning when waking I was being bitten by gigantic big blue flies that had been attracted by the fish, I was naked and they were biting like mad, which annoyed me, as the pieces of pillow had annoyed me and somehow I tied it up with Mardou's Indianness, the fish heads the awful sloppy way to dispose of fish, she sensing my annoyance but laughing, ah bird)—that alley, out there, in the dream, Adam, and in the house, the actual room and bed of Mardou and I the whole world roaring around us, back ass flat—Yuri also there, and when I turn my head (after nameless events of the millionfold mothswarms) suddenly he's got Mardou on the bed laid out and wiggling and is necking furiously with her—at first I say nothing—when I look again, again they're at it, I get mad—I'm beginning to wake up, just as I give Mardou a rabbit punch in the back of her neck, which causes Yuri to reach a hand for me—I wake up I'm swinging Yuri by the heels against the brick fireplace wall.—On waking from this dream I told all to Mardou except the part where I hit her or Yuri—and she too (in tying in with our telepathies already experienced that sad summer season now autumn mooned to death, we'd communicated many feelings of empathy and I'd come running to see her on nights when she sensed it) had been dreaming like me of the whole world around our bed, of Frank, Adam, others, her recurrent dream of her father rushing off, in a train, the spasm of almost orgasm.—"Ah honey I want to stop all this drinking these nightmares'll kill me—you don't know how jealous I was in that dream" (a feeling I'd not yet had about Mardou)—the energy behind this anxious dream had obtained from her reaction to my foolishness with the redshirt boy (Absolutely insufferable type anyway" Carmody had commented "tho obviously good-looking, really Leo you were funny" and Mardou: "Acting like a little boy but I like it.")—Her reaction had of course been violent, on arriving home, after she'd tugged me in the Mask in front of everyone including her Berkeley friends who saw her and probably even heard "It's me or him!" and the madness humor futility of that—arriving in Heavenly Lane she'd found a balloon in the hall, nice young writer John Golz who lived downstairs had been playing balloons with the kids of the Lane all day and some were in the hall, with the balloon Mardou had (drunk) danced around the floor, puffing and poooshing and flupping it up with dance interpretive gestures and said something that not only made me fear her madness, her hospital type insanity, but cut my heart deeply, and so deeply that she could not therefore have been insane, in communicating something so exactly, with precise—whatever—"You can go now I have this ballon."—"What do you mean?" (I, drunk, on floor blearing).—"I have this balloon now—I don't need you any more—goodbye—goo away—leave me alone"—a statement that even in my drunkenness made me heavy as lead and I lay there, on the floor, where I slept an hour while she played with the balloon and finally went to bed, waking me up at dawn to undress and get in—both of us dreaming the nightmare of the world around our bed—and that GUILT-Jealousy entering into my mind for the first time—the crux of this entire tale being: I want Mardou because she has begun to reject me—BECAUSE—"But baby that was a mad dream."—"I was so jealous—I was sick."—I harkened suddenly now to what Mardou'd said the first week of our relationship, when, I thought secretly, in my mind I had privately superseded her importance with the importance of my writing work, as, in every romance, the first week is so intense all previous worlds are eligible for throwover, but when the energy (of mystery, pride) begins to wane, elder worlds of sanity, well-being, common sense, etc., return, so I had secretly told myself: "My work's more important than Mardou."—Nevertheless she'd sensed it, that first week, and now said, "Leo there's something different now—

64

in you—I feel it in me—I don't know what it is." I knew very
well what it was and pretended not to be able to articulate with
myself and least of all with her anyway—I remembered now,
in the waking from the jealousy nightmare, where she necks with
Yuri, something had changed, I could sense it, something in me
was cracked, there was a new loss, a new Mardou even—and,
again, the difference was not isolated in myself who had dreamed
the cuckold dream, but in she, the subject, who'd not dreamed
it, but participated somehow in the general rueful mixed up
dream of all this life with me—so I felt she could now this
morning look at me and tell that something had died—not due
to the balloon and "You can go now"—but the dream—and so
the dream, the dream, I kept harping on it, desperately I kept
chewing and telling about it, over coffee, to her, finally when
Carmody and Adam and Yuri came (in themselves lonely and
looking to come get juices from that great current between
Mardou and me running, a current everybody I found out later
wanted to get in on, the act) I began telling *them* about the
dream, stressing, stressing, stressing the Yuri part, where Yuri
"every time I turn my back" is kissing her—naturally the others
wanting to know their parts, which I told with less vigor—a
sad Sunday afternoon, Yuri going out to get beer, a spread,
bread—eating a little—and in fact a few wrestling matches that
broke my heart. For when I saw Mardou for fun wrestling with
Adam (who was not the villain of the dream tho now I figured
I must have switched persons) I was pierced with that pain
that's now all over me, that firstpain, how cute she looked in her
jeans wrestling and struggling (I'd said "She's strong as hell,
d'jever hear of of her fight with Jack Steen? try her Adam")—
Adam having already started to wrestle with Frank on some
impetus from some talk about holds, now Adam had her pinned
in the coitus position on the floor (which in itself didn't hurt
me)—it was her beautifulness, her game guts wrestling, I felt
proud, I wanted to know how Carmody felt NOW (feeling he

65

must have been at the outset critical of her for being a Negro,
he being a Texan and a Texas gentleman-type at that) to see her
be so great, buddy like, joining in, humble and meek too and
a real woman. Even somehow the presence of Yuri, whose personality was energized already in my mind from the energy of
the dream, added to my love of Mardou—I suddenly loved her.
—They wanted me to go with them, sit in the park—as agreed
in solemn sober conclaves Mardou said "But I'll stay here and
read and do things, Leo, you go with them like we said"—as they
left and trooped down the stairs I stayed behind to tell her I
loved her now—she was not as surprised, or pleased, as I wished
—she had looked at Yuri now already with the point of view
eyes not only of my dream but had seen him in a new light as
a possible successor to me because of my continual betrayal and
getting drunk.

Yuri Gligoric: a young poet, 22, had just come down from
apple-picking Oregon, before that a waiter in a big dude ranch
dininghall—tall thin blond Yugoslavian, good-looking, very
brash and above all trying to cut Adam and myself and Carmody, all the time knowing us as an old revered trinity, wanting, naturally, as a young unpublished unknown but very genius
poet to destroy the big established gods and raise himself—
wanting therefore their women too, being uninhibited, or un-
saddened, yet, at least.—I liked him, considered him another
new "young brother" (as Leroy and Adam before, whom I'd
"shown" writing tricks) and now I would show Yuri and he
would be a buddy with me and walk around with me and Mardou
—his own lover, June, had left him, he'd treated her badly,
he wanted her back, she was with another life in Compton, I
sympathized with him and asked about the progress of his letters
and phonecalls to Compton, and, most important, as I say, he
was now for the first time suddenly looking at me and saying
"Percepied I want to talk to you—suddenly I want to really
know you."—In a joke at the Sunday wine in Dante's I'd said

"Frank's leching after Adam, Adam's leching after Yuri" and Yuri'd thrown in "And I'm leching after you."

Indeed he was indeed. On this mournful Sunday of my first pained love of Mardou after sitting in the park with the boys as agreed, I dragged myself again home, to work, to Sunday dinner, guiltily, arriving late, finding my mother glum and all-weekend-alone in a chair with her shawl . . . and my thoughts rich on Mardou now—not thinking it of any importance whatever that I had told young Yuri not only "I dreamed you were necking with Mardou" but also, at a soda fountain en route to the park when Adam wanted to call Sam and we all sat at counter waiting, with limeades, "Since I saw you last I've fallen in love with that girl," information which he received without comment and which I hope he still remembers, and of course does.

And so now brooding over her, valuing the precious good moments we'd had that heretofore I'd avoided thinking of, came the fact, ballooning in importance, the amazing fact she is the only girl I've ever known who could really understand bop and sing it, she'd said that first cuddly day of the redbulb at Adam's "While I was flipping I heard bop, on juke boxes and in the Red Drum and wherever I was happening to hear it, with an entirely new and different sense, which tho, I really can't describe."—"But what was it like?"—"But I can't describe it, it not only sent waves—went through me—I can't, like, *make* it, in telling it in words, you know? OO dee bee dee dee" singing a few notes, so cutely.—The night we walked swiftly down Larkin past the Blackhawk with Adam actually but he was following and listening, close head to head, singing wild choruses of jazz and bop, at times I'd phrase and she did perfect in fact interesting modern and advanced chords (like I'd never heard anywhere and which bore resemblance to Bartok modern chords but were hep wise to bop) and at other times she just did her chords as I did the bass fiddle, in the old great legend (again of the roaring high davenport amazing smash-afternoon which I expect

67

no one to understand) before, I'd with Ossip Popper sung bop, made records, always taking the part of the bass fiddle thum thum to his phrasing (so much I see now like Billy Eckstine's bop phrasing)—the two of us arm in arm rushing longstrides down Market the hip old apple of the California Apple singing bop and well too—the glee of it, and coming after an awful party at Roger Walker's where (Adam's arrangement and my acquiescence) instead of a regular party were just boys and all queer including one Mexican younghustler and Mardou far from being nonplused enjoyed herself and talked—nevertheless of it all, rushing home to the Third Street bus singing gleeful—

The time we read Faulkner together, I read her *Spotted Horses*, out loud—when Mike Murphy came in she told him to sit and listen as I'd go on but then I was different and I couldn't read the same and stopped—but next day in her gloomy solitude Mardou sat down and read the entire Faulkner portable.

The time we went to a French movie on Larkin, the Vogue, saw *The Lower Depths*, held hands, smoked, felt close—tho out on Market Street she would not have me hold her arm for fear people of the street there would think her a hustler, which it would look like but I felt mad but let it go and we walked along, I wanted to go into a bar for a wine, she was afraid of all the behatted men ranged at the bar, now I saw her Negro fear of American society she was always talking about but palpably in the streets which never gave me any concern—tried to console her, show her she could do anything with me, "In fact baby I'll be a famous man and you'll be the dignified wife of a famous man so don't worry" but she said "You don't understand" but her little girl-like fear so cute, so edible, I let it go, we went home, to tender love scenes together in our own and secret dark—

Fact, the time, one of those fine times when we, or that is, I didn't drink and we spent the whole night together in bed, this time telling ghost stories, the tales of Poe I could remember, then we made some up, and finally we were making madhouse eyes at each other and trying to frighten with round stares, she showed me how one of her Market Street reveries had been that she was a catatonic ("Tho then I didn't know what the word meant, but like, I walked stiffly hang arming arms hanging and man not a soul dared to speak to me and some were afraid to look, there I was walking along zombie-like and just thirteen.") (Oh gleeful shnuff-fleeflue in fluffle in her little lips, I see the outthrust teeth, I say sternly, "Mardou you must get your teeth cleaned at once, at that hospital there, the therapist, get a dentist too—it's all free so do it—" because I see beginnings of bad congestion at the corners of her pearlies which would lead to decay)—and she makes the madwoman face at me, the face rigid, the eyes shining shining shining like the stars of heaven and far from being frightened I am utterly amazed at the beauty of her and I say "And I also see the earth in your eyes that's what I think of you, you have a certain kind of beauty, not that I'm hung-up on the earth and Indians and all that and wanta harp all the time about you and us, but I see in your eyes such warm—but when you make the madwoman I don't see madness but glee glee—it's like the ragamuffin dusts in the little kid's corner and he's asleep in his crib now and I love you, rain'll fall on our eaves some day sweetheart"—and we have just candlelight so the mad acts are funnier and the ghost stories more chilling—the one about the—but a lack, a lark, I go larking in the good things and don't and do forget my pain—

Extending the eye business, the time we closed our eyes (again not drinking because of broke, poverty would have saved this romance) and I sent her messages, "Are you ready," and I see the first thing in my black eye world and ask her to describe it, amazing how we came to the same thing, it was some rapport, I saw crystal chandeliers and she saw white petals in a black bog just after some melding of images as amazing as the accurate images I'd exchange with Carmody in Mexico—Mardou and I both seeing the same thing, some madness shape, some fountain, now by me forgotten and really not important yet, come together in mutual descriptions of it and joy and glee in this telepathic triumph of ours, ending where our thoughts meet at the crystal white and petals, the mystery—I see the gleeful hunger of her face devouring the sight of mine, I could die, don't break my heart radio with beautiful music, O world—the candlelight again, flickering, I'd bought a slue of candles in the store, the corners of our room in darkness, her shadow naked brown as she hurries to the sink—our use of the sink—my fear of communicating WHITE images to her in our telepathies for fear she'll be (in her fun) reminded of our racial difference, at that time making me feel guilty, now I realize it was one love's gentility on my part—Lord.

The good ones—going up on the top of Nob Hill at night with a fifth of Royal Chalice Tokay, sweet, rich, potent, the lights of the city and of the bay beneath us, the sad mystery—sitting on a bench there, lovers, loners pass, we pass the bottle, talk—she tells all her little girlhood in Oakland.—It's like Paris—it's soft, the breeze blows, the city may swelter but the hillers do fly—and over the bay is Oakland (ah me Hart Crane Melville and all ye assorted brother poets of the American night that once I thought would be my sacrificial altar and now it is but who's to care, know, and I lost love because of it—drunkard, dullard, poet)—returning via Van Ness to Aquatic Park beach, sitting in the sand, as I pass Mexicans I feel that great hepness I'd been having all summer on the street with Mardou my old dream of wanting to be vital, alive like a Negro or an Indian or a Denver Jap or a New York Puerto Rican come true, with her by my side so young, sexy; slender, strange, hip, myself in jeans and casual and both of us as if young (I say as if, to my 31)—the cops telling us to leave the beach, a lonely Negro passing us twice and staring—we walk along the waterslap, she laughs to see the crazy figures of reflected light of the moon dancing so bug-like

70

in the ululating cool smooth water of the night—we smell harbors, we dance—

The time I walked her in broad sweet dry Mexico plateau-like or Arizona-like morning to her appointment with therapist at the hospital, along the Embarcadero, denying the bus, hand in hand—I proud, thinking, "In Mexico she'll look just like this and not a soul'll know I'm not an Indian by God and we'll go along"—and I point out the purity and clarity of the clouds, "Just like Mexico honey, O you'll love it" and we go up the busy street to the big grimbrick hospital and I'm supposed to be going home from there but she lingers, sad smile, love smile, when I give in and agree to wait for her 20-minute interview and her coming out she radiantly breaks out glad and rushes to the gate which we've already passed in her almost therapy-giving-up strolling-with-me meandering, men—love—not for sale—my prize—possession—nobody gets it but gets a Sicilian line down his middle—a German boot in the kisser, an axe Canuck—I'll pin them wriggling poets to some London wall right here, explained.—And as I wait for her to come out, I sit on side of water, in Mexico-like gravel and grass and concrete blocks and take out sketchbooks and draw big word pictures of the skyline and of the bay, putting in a little mention of the great fact of the huge all-world with its infinite levels, from Standard Oil top down to waterslap at barges where old bargemen dream, the difference between men, the difference so vast between concerns of executives in skyscrapers and seadogs on harbor and psychoanalysts in stuffy offices in great grim buildings full of dead bodies in the morgue below and madwomen at windows, hoping thereby to instill in Mardou recognition of fact it's a big world and psychoanalysis is a small way to explain it since it only scratches the surface, which is, analysis, cause and effect, why instead of what—when she comes out I read it to her, not impressing her too much but she loves me, holds my hand as we cut down along Embarcadero towards her place and when I leave her at Third and Townsend train in warm clear afternoon she says "O I hate to see you go, I really miss you now."—"But I gotta be home in time to make the supper—and write— so honey I'll be back, tomorrow remember promptly at ten."—And tomorrow I arrive at midnight instead.

The time we had a shuddering come together and she said "I was lost suddenly" and she was lost with me tho not coming herself but frantic in my franticness (Reich's beclouding of the senses) and how she loved it—all our teachings in bed, I explain me to her, she explains her to me, we work, we wail, we bop— we throw clothes off and jump at each other (after always her little trip to the diaphragm sink and I have to wait holding softer and making goofy remarks and she laughs and trickles water) then here she comes padding to me across the Garden of Eden, and I reach up and help her down to my side on the soft bed, I pull her little body to me and it is warm, her warm spot is hot, I kiss her brown breasts both of them, I kiss her loveshoulders—she keeps with her lips going "ps ps ps" little kiss sounds where actually no contact is made with my face except when haphazardly while doing something else I do move it against her and her little ps ps kisses connect and are as sad and soft as when they don't—it's her little litany of night—and when she's sick and we're worried, then she takes me on her, on her arm, on mine—she services the mad unthinking beast—I spend long nights and many hours making her, finally I have her, I pray for it to come, I can hear her breathing harder, I hope against hope it's time, a noise in the hall (or whoop of drunkards next door) takes her mind off and she can't make it and laughs —but when she does make it I hear her crying, whimpering, the shuddering electrical female orgasm makes her sound like a little girl crying, moaning in the night, it lasts a good twenty seconds and when it's over she moans, "O why can't it last longer," and, "O when will I when you do?"—"Soon now I bet," I say, "you're getting closer and closer"—sweating against her in the

warm sad Frisco with its damn old scows mooing on the tide
out there, voom, voooom, and stars flickering on the water even
where it waves beneath the pierhead where you expect gangsters
dropping encemented bodies, or rats, or The Shadow—my little
Mardou whom I love, who'd never read my unpublished works
but only the first novel, which has guts but has a dreary prose
to it when all's said and done and so now holding her and
spent with sex I dream of the day she'll read great works
by me and admire me, remembering the time Adam had said
in sudden strangeness in his kitchen, "Mardou, what do you
really think of Leo and myself as writers, our positions in the
world, the rack of time," asking her that, knowing that her
thinking is in accord in some ways more or less with the subterraneans whom he admires and fears, whose opinions he values
with wonder—Mardou not really replying but evading the issue,
but old man me plots greatbooks for her amaze—all those good
things, good times we had, others I am now in the heat of my
frenzy forgetting but I must tell all, but angels know all and
record it in books—

But think of all the bad times—I have a list of bad times to
make the good times, the times I was good to her and like I
should be, to make it sick—when early in our love I was three
hours late which is a lot of hours of lateness for younglovers, and
so she wigged, got frightened, walked around the church handsapockets brooding looking for me in the mist of dawn and I
ran out (seeing her note saying "I am gone out to look for
you") (in all Frisco yet! that east and west, north and south of
soulless loveless bleak she'd seen from the fence, all the count-
less men in hats going into buses and not caring about the naked
girl on the fence, why)—when I saw her, I myself running out to
find her, I opened my arms a halfmile away—

The worst almost worst time of all when a red flame crossed
my brain, I was sitting with her and Larry O'Hara in his pad,
we'd been drinking French Bordeaux and blasting, a subject was

up, I had a hand on Larry's knee shouting "But listen to me, but listen to me!" wanting to make my point so bad there was a big crazy plead in the tone and Larry deeply engrossed in what Mardou is saying simultaneously and feeding a few words to her dialog, in the emptiness after the red flame I suddenly leap up and rush to the door and tug at it, ugh, locked, the in-door chain lock, I slide and undo it and with another try I lunge out in the hall and down the stairs as fast as my thieves' quick crepesoul shoes'll take me, putt pitterpit, floor after floor reeling around me as I round the stairwell, leaving them agape up there —calling back in half hour, meeting her on the street three blocks away—there is no hope—

The time even when we'd agreed she needed money for food, that I'd go home and get it and just bring it back and stay a short while, but I'm at this time far from in love, but bugged, not only her pitiful demands for money but that doubt, that old Mardou-doubt, and so rush into her pad, Alice her friend is there, I use that as an excuse (because Alice dike-like silent unpleasant and strange and likes no one) to lay the two bills on Mardou's dishes at sink, kiss a quick peck in the malt of her ear, say "I'll be back tomorrow" and run right out again without even asking her opinion—as if the whore'd made me for two bucks and I was sore.

How clear the realization one is going mad—the mind has a silence, nothing happens in the physique, urine gathers in your loins, your ribs contract.

Bad time she asked me, "What does Adam really think of me, you never told me, I know he resents us together but—" and I told her substantially what Adam had told me, of which none should have been divulged to her for the sake of her peace of mind, "He said it was just a social question of his not now wanting to get hung-up with you lovewise because you're Negro" —feeling again her telepathic little shock cross the room to me, it sunk deep, I question my motives for telling her this.

The time her cheerful little neighbor young writer John Golz came up (he dutifully eight hours a day types working on magazine stories, admirer of Hemingway, often feeds Mardou and is a nice Indiana boy and means no harm and certainly not a slinky snaky interesting subterranean but openfaced, jovial, plays with children in the court for God's sake)—came up to see Mardou, I was there alone (for some reason, Mardou at a bar with our accord arrangement, the night she went out with a Negro boy she didn't like too much but just for fun and told Adam she was doing it because she wanted to make it with a Negro boy again, which made me jealous, but Adam said "If I should if she should hear that you went out with a white girl to see if you could make it again she'd sure be flattered, Leo")— that night, I was at her place waiting, reading, young John Golz came in to borrow cigarettes and seeing I was alone wanted to talk literature—"Well I believe that the most important thing is selectivity," and I blew up and said "Ah don't give me all that high school stuff I've heard it and heard it long before you were born almost for krissakes and really now, say something interesting and new about writing"—putting him down, sullen, for reasons mainly of irritation and because he seemed harmless and therefore could be counted on to be safe to yell at, which he was—putting him down, her friend, was not nice—no, the world's no fit place for this kind of activity, and what we gonna do, and where? when? wha wha wha, the baby bawls in the midnight boom.

Nor could it have been charming and helpful to her fears and anxieties to have me start out, at the outset of our romance, "kissing her down between the stems"—starting and then suddenly quitting so later in an unguarded drinkingmoment she said, "You suddenly stopped as tho I was—" and the reason I stopped being in itself not as significant as the reason I did it at all, to secure her greater sexual interest, which once tied on with a bow knot, I could dally out of—the warm lovemouth of the woman,

the womb, being the place for men who love, not . . . this im-
mature drunkard and egomaniacal . . . this . . . knowing as I do
from past experience and interior sense, you've got to fall down
on your knees and beg the woman's permission, beg the woman's
forgiveness for all your sins, protect her, support her, doing
everything for her, die for her but for God's sake love her and
love her all the way in and every way you can—yes psychoanalysis, I hear (fearing secretly the few times I had come into contact with the rough stubble-like quality of the pubic, which was
Negroid and therefore a little rougher, tho not enough to make
any difference, and the insides itself I should say the best, the
richest, most fecund moist warm and full of hidden soft slidy
mountains, also the pull and force of the muscles being so power-
ful she unknowing often vice-like closes over and makes a dam-
up and hurt, tho this I only realized the other night, too late—).
And so the final lingering physiological doubt I have that this
contraction and greatstrength of womb, responsible I think now
in retrospect for the time when Adam in his first encounter with
her experienced piercing unsupportable screamingsudden pain,
so he had to go to the doctor and have himself bandaged and all
(and even later when Carmody arrived and made a local orgone
accumulator out of a big old watercan and burlap and vegetative
materials placing the nozzle of himself into the nozzle of the can
to heal), I now wonder and suspect if our little chick didn't really
intend to bust us in half, if Adam isn't thinking it's his own fault
and doesn't know, but she contracted mightily there (the lesbian!) (always knew it) and busted him and fixed him and
couldn't do it to me but tried enough till she threw me over a
dead hulk that now I am—psychoanalyst, I'm serious!

It's too much. Beginning, as I say with the pushcart incident
—the night we drank red wine at Dante's and were in a drinking
mood now both of us so disgusted—Yuri came with us, Ross Wallenstein was in there and maybe to show off to Mardou Yuri acted

like a kid all night and kept hitting Wallenstein on the back of
his head with little finger taps like goofing in a bar but Wallenstein (who's always being beaten up by hoodlums because of
this) turned around a stiff death's-head gaze with big eyes glaring
behind glasses, his Christlike blue unshaven cheeks, staring rig-
idly as tho the stare itself will floor Yuri, not speaking for a
long time, finally saying, "Man, don't bug me," and turning back
to his conversation with friends and Yuri does it again and Ross
turns again the same pitiless awful subterranean sort of non-
violent Indian Mahatma Gandhi defense of some kind (which
I'd suspected that first time he talked to me saying, "Are you
a fag you talk like a fag" a remark coming from him so absurd
because so inflammable and me 170 pounds to his 130 or 120
for God's sake so I thought secretly "No you can't fight this
man he will only scream and yell and call cops and let you hit
him again and haunt all your dreams, there is no way to put a
subterranean down on the floor or for that matter put em down
at all, they are the most unputdownable in this world and new cul-
ture")—finally Wallenstein going to the head for a leak and
Yuri says to me, Mardou being at the bar gathering three more
wines, "Come on let's go in the john and bust him up," and I
get up to go with Yuri but not to bust up Ross rather to stop
anything might happen there—Yuri having been in his own
in fact realer way than mine almost a hoodlum, imprisoned in
Soledad for defending himself in some vicious fight in reform
school—Mardou stopping us both as we head to the head, saying,
"My God if I hadn't stopped you" (laughing embarrassed little
Mardou smile and shniffle) "you'd actually have gone in there"
—a former love of Ross's and now the bottomless toilet of Ross's
position in her affections I think probably equal to mine now,
O damblast the thorny flaps of the pap time page—
    Going thence to the Mask as usual, beers, get worse drunk, then
out to walk home, Yuri having just arrived from Oregon having
no place to sleep is asking if it's allright to sleep at our place, I

77

let Mardou speak for her own house, tho feebly say some "okay" in the middle of the confusion, and Yuri comes heading homeward with us—en route finds a pushcart, says "Get in, I'll be a taxicab and push you both home up the hill."—Okay we get in, and lie on our backs drunk as only you can get drunk on red wine, and he pushes us from the Beach at that fateful park (where we'd sat that first sad Sunday afternoon of my dream and premonitions) and we ride along in the pushcart of eternity, Angel Yuri pushing it, I can only see stars and occasional rooftops of blocks—no thought in any mind (except briefly in mine, possibly in others) of the sin, the loss entailed for the poor Italian beggar losing his cart there—on down Broadway clear to Mardou's, in the pushcart, at one point I push and they ride, Mardou and I singing bop and also bop to the tune *Are the Stars out Tonight* and just drunk—parking it foolishly in front of Adam's and rushing up, making noise.—Next day, after sleeping on floor with Yuri snoring on the couch, waiting up for Adam as if beaming to hear told about our exploit, Adam comes home blackfaced mad from work and says "Really you have no idea the pain you're causin' some poor old Armenian peddler you never think that—but jeopardizing my pad with that thing in front, supposing the cops find it, and what's the matter with you." And Carmody saying to me "Leo I think you perpetrated this masterpiece" or "You masterminded this brilliant move" or such which I really didn't—and all day we've been cutting up and down stairs looking at pushcart which far from being cop-discovered still sits there but with Adam's landlord teetering in front of it, waiting to see who's going to claim it, sensing something fishy, and of all things Mardou's poor purse still in it where drunkenly we'd left it and the landlord finally confiscating IT and waiting for further development (she lost a few dollars and her only purse).—"Only thing that can happen, Adam, is the cops'll find the pushcart, they can very well see the purse, the address, and take it to Mardou's but all she has to say is 'O I found my purse,' and that's that, and nothing'll happen." But Adam cries, "O you even if nothing'll happen you screw up the security of my pad, come in making noise, leave a licensed vehicle out front, and tell me nothing'll happen."— And I had sensed he'd be mad and am prepared and say, "To hell with that, you can give hell to these but you won't give hell to me, I won't take it from you—that was just a drunken prank," I add, and Adam says, "This is my house and I can get mad when it's—" so I up and throw his keys (the keys he'd had made for me to walk in and out any time) at him but they're entwined with the chain of my mother's keys and for a moment we fumble seriously at the mixed keys on the floor disengaging them and he gets his and I say "No that, that's mine, there," and he puts it in his pocket and there we are.—I want to rush up and leave, like at Larry's.—Mardou is there seeing me flip again—far from helping her from flips. (Once she'd asked me "If I ever flip what will you do, will you help me?—Supposing I think you're trying to harm me?"—"Honey," I said, "I'll try in fact I'll reassure you I'm not harming you and you'd come to your senses, I'll protect you," the confidence of the old man—but in reality himself flipping more often.)—I feel great waves of dark hostility, I mean hate, malice, destructiveness flowing out of Adam in his corner chair, I can hardly sit under the withering telepathic blast and there's all that *yage* of Carmody's around the pad, in suitcases, it's too much—(it's a comedy tho, we agree it will be a comedy later)—we talk of other things—Adam suddenly flips the key back at me, it lands in my thighs, and instead of dangling it in my finger (as if considering, as if a wily Canuck calculating advantages) I boy-like jump up and throw the key back in my pocket with a little giggle, to make Adam feel better, also to impress Mardou with my "fairness"—but she never noticed, was watching something else—so now that peace is restored I say "And in any case it was Yuri's fault it isn't at all as Frank says my unqualified masterminding"—(this pushcart, this darkness,

79

the same as when Adam in the prophetic dream descended the wood steps to see the "Russian Patriarch", there were pushcarts there)—So in the letter that I write to Mardou answering her beauty which I have paraphrased, I make stupid angry but "pretending to be fair," "to be calm, deep, poetic" statements, like, "Yes, I got mad and threw Adam's keys back at him, because 'friendship, admiration, poetry sleep in the respectful mystery' and the invisible world is too beatific to have to be dragged before the court of social realities," or some such twaddle that Mardou must have glanced at with one eye—the letter, which was supposed to match the warmth of hers, her cuddly-in-October masterpiece, beginning with the inane-if-at-all confession: "The last time I wrote a love note it turned out to be boloney" (referring to an earlier in the year half-romance with Arlene Wohlstetter) "and I am glad you are honest," or "have honest eyes," the next sentence said—the letter intended to arrive Saturday morning to make her feel my warm presence while I was out taking my hardworking and deserving mother to her bi-six-monthlial show and shopping on Market Street (old Canuck workingwoman completely ignorant of arrangement of mingled streets of San Francisco) but arriving long after I saw her and read while I was there, and dull—this not a literary complaint, but something that must have pained Mardou, the lack of reciprocity and the stupidity regarding my attack at Adam— "Man, you had no right to yell at him, really, it's his pad, his right"—but the letter a big defense of this "right to yell at Adam" and not at all response to her love notes—

The pushcart incident not important in itself, but what I saw, what my quick eye and hungry paranoia ate—a gesture of Mardou's that made my heart sink even as I doubted maybe I wasn't seeing, interpreting right, as so oft I do.—We'd come in and run upstairs and jumped on the big double bed waking Adam up and yelling and tousling and Carmody too sitting on the edge as if to say "Now children now children," just a lot of drunken

lushes—at one time in the play back and forth between the
rooms Mardou and Yuri ended on the couch together in front,
where I think all three of us had flopped—but I ran to the bedroom for further business, talking, coming back I saw Yuri who
knew I was coming flop off the couch onto the floor and as he
did so Mardou (who probably didn't know I was coming) shot
out her hand at him as if to say OH YOU RASCAL as if almost
he'd before rolling off the couch goosed her or done something
playful—I saw for the first time their youthful playfulness which
I in my scowlingness and writer-ness had not participated in and
my old man-ness about which I kept telling myself "You're old
you old sonofabitch you're lucky to have such a young sweet
thing" (while nevertheless at the same time plotting, as I'd been
doing for about three weeks now, to get rid of Mardou, without
her being hurt, even if possible "without her noticing" so as to
get back to more comfortable modes of life, like say, stay at
home all week and write and work on the three novels to make
a lot of money and come in to town only for good times if not
to see Mardou then any other chick will do, this was my three
week thought and really the energy behind or the surface one
behind the creation of the Jealousy Phantasy in the Gray Guilt
dream of the World Around Our Bed)—now I saw Mardou
pushing Yuri with a O H Y O U and I shuddered to think
something maybe was going on behind my back—felt warned
too by the quick and immediate manner Yuri heard me coming
and rolled off but as if guiltily as I say after some kind of
goose or feel up some illegal touch of Mardou which made
her purse little love loff lips at him and push at him and
like kids.—Mardou was just like a kid I remember the first
night I met her when Julien, rolling joints on the floor, she
behind him hunched, I'd explained to them why that week I
wasn't drinking at all (true at the time, and due to events on
the ship in New York, scaring me, saying to myself "If you
keep on drinking like that you'll die you can't even hold a simple

job any more," so returning to Frisco and not drinking at all and everybody exclaiming "O you look wonderful"), telling that first night almost heads together with Mardou and Julien, they so kidlike in their naive WHY when I told them I wasn't drinking any more, so kidlike listening to my explanation about the one can of beer leading to the second, the sudden gut explosions and glitters, the third can, the fourth, "And then I go off and drink for days and I'm gone man, like, I'm afraid I'm an alcoholic" and they kidlike and othergenerationey making no comment, but awed, curious—in the same rapport with young Yuri here (her age) pushing at him, Oh You, which in drunkenness I paid not too much attention to, and we slept, Mardou and I on the floor, Yuri on the couch (so kidlike, indulgent, funny of him, all that) —this first exposure of the realization of the mysteries of the guilt jealousy dream leading, from the pushcart time, to the night we went to Bromberg's, most awful of all.

Beginning as usual in the Mask.

Nights that begin so glitter clear with hope, let's go see our friends, things, phones ring, people come and go, coats, hats, statements, bright reports, metropolitan excitements, a round of beers, another round of beers, the talk gets more beautiful, more excited, flushed, another round, the midnight hour, later, the flushed happy faces are now wild and soon there's the swaying buddy da day oobab bab smash smoke drunken latenight goof leading finally to the bartender, like a seer in Eliot, TIME TO CLOSE UP—in this manner more or less arriving at the Mask where a kid called Harold Sand came in, a chance acquaintance of Mardou's from a year ago, a young novelist looking like Leslie Howard who'd just had a manuscript accepted and so acquired a strange grace in my eyes I wanted to devour— interested in him for same reasons as Lavalina, literary avidity, envy—as usual paying less attention therefore to Mardou (at table) than Yuri whose continual presence with us now did not raise my suspicions, whose complaints "I don't have a place to stay—do you realize Percepied what it is not to even have a place to write? I have not girls, nothing, Carmody and Moorad won't let me stay up there any more, they're a couple of old sisters," not sinking in, and already the only comment I'd made to Mardou about Yuri had been, after his leaving, "He's just like that Mexican stud comes up here and grabs up your last cigarettes," both of us laughing because whenever she was at her lowest financial ebb, bang, somebody who needed a "mooch" was there—not that I would call Yuri a mooch in the least (I'll tread lightly on him on this point, for obvious reasons).—(Yuri and I'd had a long talk that week in a bar, over port wines, he claimed everything was poetry, I tried to make the common old distinction between verse and prose, he said, "Lissen Percepied do you believe in freedom?—then say what you want, it's poetry, poetry, all of it is poetry, great prose is poetry, great verse is poetry."—"Yes" I said "but verse is verse and prose is prose." —"No no" he yelled "it's all poetry."—"Okay," I said, "I believe in you believing in freedom and maybe you're right, have another wine." And he read me his "best line" which was something to do with "seldom nocturne" that I said sounded like small magazine poetry and wasn't his best—as already I'd seen some much better poetry by him concerning his tough boyhood, about cats, mothers in gutters, Jesus striding in the ashcan, appearing incarnate shining on the blowers of slum tenements or that is making great steps across the light—the sum of it something he could do, and did, well—"No, seldom nocturne isn't your meat" but he claimed it was great, "I would say rather it was great if you'd written it suddenly on the spur of the moment."—"But I did—right out of my mind it flowed and I threw it down, it sounds like it's been planned but it wasn't, it was bang! just like you say, spontaneous vision!"— Which I now doubt tho his saying "seldom nocturne" came to him spontaneously made me suddenly respect it more, some falsehood hiding beneath our wine yells in a saloon on Kearney.)

83

Yuri hanging out with Mardou and me every night almost—like a shadow—and knowing Sand himself from before, so he, Sand, walking into the Mask, flushed successful young author but "ironic" looking and with a big parkingticket sticking out of his coat lapel, was set upon by the three of us with avidity, made to sit at our table—made to talk.—Around the corner from Mask to 13 Pater thence the lot of us going, and en route (reminiscent now more strongly and now with hints of pain of the pushcart night and Mardou's OH YOU) Yuri and Mardou start racing, pushing, shoving, wrestling on the sidewalk and finally she lofts a big empty cardboard box and throws it at him and he throws it back, they're like kids again—I walk on ahead in serious tone conversation with Sand tho—he too has eyes for Mardou—somehow I'm not able (at least haven't tried) to communicate to him that she is my love and I would prefer if he didn't have eyes for her so obviously, just as Jimmy Lowell, a colored seaman who'd suddenly phoned in the midst of an Adam party, and came, with a Scandinavian shipmate, looking at Mardou and me wondering, asking me "Do you make it with her sex?" and I saying yes and the night after the Red Drum session where Art Blakey was whaling like mad and Thelonious Monk sweating leading the generation with his elbow chords, eying the band madly to lead them on, *the monk and saint of bop* I kept telling Yuri, smooth sharp hep Jimmy Lowell leans to me and says "I would like to make it with your chick," (like in the old days Leroy and I always swapping so I'm not shocked), "would it be okay if I asked her?" and I saying "She's not that kind of girl, I'm sure she believes in one at a time, if you ask her that's what she'll tell you man" (at that time still feeling no pain or jealousy, this incidentally the night before the Jealousy Dream)—not able to communicate to Lowell that's—that I wanted her—to stay—to be stammer stammer be mine—not being able to come right out and say, "Lissen this is my girl, what are you talking about, if you want to try to make her you'll

84

have to tangle with me, you understand that pops as well as I
do."—In that way with a stud, in another way with polite dignified Sand a very interesting young fellow, like, "Sand, Mardou
is my girl and I would prefer, etc."—but he has eyes for her
and the reason he stays with us and goes around the corner to
13 Pater, but it's Yuri starts wrestling with her and goofing in
the streets—so when we leave 13 Pater later on (a dike bar
slummish now and nothing to it, where a year ago there were
angels in red shirts straight out of Genet and Djuna Barnes) I
get in the front seat of Sand's old car, he's going at least to drive
us home, I sit next to him at the clutch in front for purposes
of talking better and in drunkenness again avoiding Mardou's
womanness, leaving room for her to sit beside me at front window
—instead of which, no sooner plops her ass behind me, jumps
over seat and dives into backseat with Yuri who is alone back
there, to wrestle again and goof with him and now with such
intensity I'm afraid to look back and see with my own eyes
what's happening and how the dream (the dream I announced
to everyone and made big issues of and told even Yuri about)
is coming true.

We pull up at Mardou's door at Heavenly Lane and drunkly
now she says (Sand and I having decided drunkenly to drive
down to Los Altos the lot of us and crash in on old Austin
Bromberg and have big further parties) "If you're going down
to Bromberg's in Los Altos you two go out, Yuri and I'll stay
here"—my heart sank deep—it sank so I gloated to hear it
for the first time and the confirmation of it crowned me and
blessed me.

And I thought, "Well boy here's your chance to get rid of
her" (which I'd plotted for three weeks now) but the sound of
this in my own ears sounded awfully false, I didn't believe it,
myself, any more.

But on the sidewalk going in flushed Yuri takes my arm as
Mardou and Sand go on ahead up the fish head stairs, "Lissen,

Leo I don't want to make Mardou at all, she's all over me, I
want you to know that I don't want to make her, all I want to
do if you're going out there is go to sleep in your bed because
I have an appointment tomorrow."—But now I myself feel reluctant to stay in Heavenly Lane for the night because Yuri will
be there, in fact now is already on the bed tacitly as if, one
would have to say, "Get off the bed so we can get in, go to that
uncomfortable chair for the night."—So this more than anything
else (in my tiredness and growing wisdom and patience) makes
me agree with Sand (also reluctant) that we might as well drive
down to Los Altos and wake up good old Bromberg, and I turn
to Mardou with eyes saying or suggesting, "You can stay with
Yuri you bitch" but she's already got her little traveling basket
or weekend bag and is putting my toothbrush hairbrush and her
things in and the idea is we three drive out—which we do,
leaving Yuri in the bed.—En route, at near Bayshore in the great
highway roadlamp night, which is now nothing but a bleakness
for me and the prospect of the "weekend" at Bromberg's a horror
of shame, I can't stand it any more and look at Mardou as soon
as Sand gets out to buy hamburgs in the diner, "You jumped in
the backseat with Yuri why'd you do that? and why'd you say
you wanted to stay with him?"—"It was silly of me, I was just
high baby." But I don't darkly any more now want to believe
her—art is short, life is long—now I've got in full dragon bloom
the monster of jealousy as green as in any cliché cartoon rising
in my being, "You and Yuri play together all the time, it's just
like the dream I told you about, that's what's horrible—O I'll
never believe in dreams come true again."—"But baby it isn't
anything like that" but I don't believe her—I can tell by looking at her she's got eyes for the youth—you can't fool an
old hand who at the age of sixteen before even the juice was
wiped off his heart by the Great Imperial World Wiper with
Sadcloth fell in love with an impossible flirt and cheater, this is
a boast—I feel so sick I can't stand it, curl up in the back seat,

alone—they drive on, and Sand having anticipated a gay talk-ative weekend now finds himself with a couple of grim lover worriers, hears in fact the fragment "But I didn't mean you to think that baby" so obviously harkening to his mind the Yuri incident—finds himself with this pair of bores and has to drive all the way down to Los Altos, and so with the same grit that made him write the half million words of his novel bends to it and pushes the car through the Peninsula night and on into the dawn.

Arriving at Bromberg's house in Los Altos at gray dawn, parking, and ringing the doorbell the three of us sheepishly I most sheepish of all—and Bromberg comes right down, at once, with great roars of approval cries "Leo I didn't know you knew each other" (meaning Sand, whom Bromberg admired very much) and in we go to rum and coffee in the crazy famous Bromberg kitchen.—You might say, Bromberg the most amazing guy in the world with small dark curly hair like the hip girl Roxanne making little garter snakes over his brow and his great really angelic eyes shining, rolling, a big burbling baby, a great genius of talk really, wrote research and essays and has (and is famous for) the greatest possible private library in the world, right there in that house, library due to his erudition and this no reflection also on his big income—the house inherited from father—was also the sudden new bosom friend of Carmody and about to go to Peru with him, they'd go dig Indian boys and talk about it and discuss art and visit literaries and things of that nature, all matters so much had been dinning in Mardou's ear (queer, cultured matters) in her love affair with me that by now she was quite tired of cultured tones and fancy explicity, emphatic daintiness of expression, of which roll-eyed ecstatic almost spastic big Bromberg almost the pastmaster, "O my dear it's such a charming thing and I think much MUCH better than the Gascoyne translation tho I do believe—" and Sand imitating him to a T, from some recent great meeting and mutual admi-

ration—so the two of them there in the once-to-me adventurous
gray dawn of the Metropolitan Great-Rome Frisco talking of
literary and musical and artistic matters, the kitchen littered,
Bromberg rushing up (in pajamas) to fetch three-inch thick
French editions of Genet or old editions of Chaucer or whatever
he and Sand'd come to, Mardou darklashed and still thinking of
Yuri (as I'm thinking to myself) sitting at the corner of the
kitchen table, with her getting-cold rum and coffee—O I on a
stool, hurt, broken, injured, about to get worse, drinking cup
after cup and loading up on the great heavy brew—the birds
beginning to sing finally at about eight and Bromberg's great
voice, one of the mightiest you can hear, making the walls of the
kitchen throw back great shudders of deep ecstatic sound—
turning on the phonograph, an expensive well-furnished completely appointed house, with French wine, refrigerators, three-
speed machines with speakers, cellar, etc.—I want to look at
Mardou I don't know with what expression—I am afraid in fact to
look only to find there the supplication in her eyes saying "Don't
worry baby, I told you, I confessed to you I was silly, I'm sorry
sorry sorry—" that "I'm-sorry" look hurting me the most as I
glance side eyes to see it. . . .

It won't do when the very bluebirds are bleak, which I mention
to Bromberg, he asking, "Whatsamatter with you this morning
Leo?" (with burbling peek under eyebrows to see me better and
make me laugh).—"Nothing, Austin, just that when I look out
the window this morning the birds are bleak."—(And earlier
when Mardou went upstairs to toilet I did mention, bearded,
gaunt, foolish drunkard, to these erudite gentlemen, something
about 'inconstancy,' which must have surprised them tho)—O
inconstancy!

So they try anyway to make the best of it in spite of my
palpable unhappy brooding all over the place, while listening
to Verdi and Puccini opera recordings in the great upstairs
library (four walls from rug to ceiling with things like *The Ex-*

planation of the Apocalypse in three volumes, the complete works
and poems of Chris Smart, the complete this and that, the apology
of so-and-so written obscurely to you-know-who in 1839, in 1638
—). I jump at the chance to say, "I'm going to sleep," it's now
eleven, I have a right to be tired, been sitting on the floor and
Mardou with dame-like majesty all this time in the easy chair
in the corner of the library (where once I'd seen the famous
one-armed Nick Spain sit when Bromberg on a happier early
time in the year played for us the original recording of *The
Rake's Progress*) and looking so, herself, tragic, lost—hurt so
much by my hurt—by my sorriness from her sorriness borrowing
—I think sensitive—that at one point in a burst of forgiveness,
need, I run and sit at her feet and lean head on her knee in
front of the others who by now don't care any more, that is Sand
does not care about these things now, deeply engrossed in the
music, the books, the brilliant conversation (the likes of which
cannot be surpassed anywhere in the world, incidentally, and
this too, tho now tiredly, crosses by my epic-wanting brain and
I see the scheme of all my life, all acquaintances, loves, worries,
travels rising again in a big symphonic mass but now I'm beginning not to care so much any more because of this 105 pounds
of woman and brown at that whose little toenails, red in the
thonged sandals, make my throat gulp)—"O dear Leo, you DO
seem to be bored."—"Not bored! how could I be bored here!"
—I wish I had some sympathetic way to tell Bromberg, "Every
time I come here there's something wrong with me, it must seem
like some awful comment on your house and hospitality and it
isn't at all, can't you understand that this morning my heart is
broken and out the window is bleak" (and how explain to him
the other time I was a guest at his place, again uninvited but
breaking in at gray dawn with Charley Krasner and the kids
were there, and Mary, and the others came, gin and Schweppes,
I became so drunk, disorderly, lost, I then too brooded and slept
in fact on the floor in the middle of the room in front of every-

body in the height of day—and for reasons so far removed from now, tho still as tho an adverse comment on the quality of Bromberg's weekend)—"No Austin I'm just sick—." No doubt, too, Sand must have hipped him quietly in a whisper somewhere what was happening with the lovers, Mardou also being silent —one of the strangest guests ever to hit Bromberg's, a poor subterranean beat Negro girl with no clothes on her back worth a twopenny (I saw to that generously), and yet so strange faced, solemn, serious, like a funny solemn unwanted probably angel in the house—feeling, as she told me, later, really unwanted because of the circumstances.—So I cop out, from the lot, from life, all of it, go to sleep in the bedroom (where Charley and I that earlier time had danced the mambo naked with Mary) and fall exhausted into new nightmares waking up about three hours later, in the heartbreakingly pure, clear, sane, happy afternoon, birds still singing, now kids singing, as if I was a spider waking up in a dusty bin and the world wasn't for me but for other airier creatures and more constant themselves and also less liable to the stains of inconstancy too—

While sleeping they three get in Sand's car and (properly) drive out to the beach, twenty miles, the boys jump in, swim, Mardou wanders on the shores of eternity her toes and feet that I love pressing down in the pale sand against the little shells and anemones and paupered dry seaweed long washed up and the wind blowing back her short haircut, as if Eternity'd met Heavenly Lane (as I thought of it in my bed) (seeing her also wandering around pouting, not knowing what to do next, abandoned by Suffering Leo and really alone and incapable of chatting about every tom dick and harry in art with Bromberg and Sand, what to do?)—So when they return she comes to the bed (after Bromberg's preliminary wild bound up the stairs and bursting in of door and "WAKE up Leo you don't want to sleep all day we've been to the beach, really it's not fair!") —"Leo," says Mardou, "I didn't want to sleep with you because

90

I didn't want to wake up in Bromberg's bed at seven o'clock in
the evening, it would be too much to cope with, I can't—" meaning her therapy (which she hadn't been going to any more out
of sheer paralysis with me and my gang and cups), her inadequacy, the great now-crushing weight and fear of madness
increasing in this disorderly awful life and unloved affair with me,
to wake up horrified from hangover in a stranger's (a kind but
nevertheless not altogether wholeheartedwelcoming stranger's)
bed, with poor incapable Leo.—I suddenly looked at her, listening not to these real poor pleas so much as digging in her eyes
that light that had shined on Yuri and it wasn't her fault it could
shine on all the world all the time, my light o love—
    "Are you sincere?"—("God you frighten me," she said later,
"you make me think suddenly I've been two people and betrayed
you in one way, with one person, and this other person—it
really frightened me—") but as I ask that, "Are you sincere?"
the pain I feel is so great, it has just risen fresh from that dis-
ordered roaring dream ("God is so disposed as to make our
lives less cruel than our dreams," is a quote I saw the other day
God knows where)—feeling all that and harkening to other
horrified hangover awakenings in Bromberg's and all the hangover awakenings in my life, feeling now, "Boy, this is the real
real beginning of the end, you can't go on much further, how
much more vagueness can your positive flesh take and how long
will it stay positive if your psyche keeps blamming on it—boy,
you are going to die, when birds get bleak—that's the sign—."
But thinking more roars than that, visions of my work neglected,
my well-being (so-called old well-being again) smashed, brain
permanently injured now—ideas for working on the railroad—O
God the whole host and foolish illusion and entire rigamarole
and madness that we erect in the place of onelove, in our sadness
—but now with Mardou leaning over me, tired, solemn, somber,
capable as she played with the little unshaven uglies of my chin
of seeing right through my flesh into my horror and capable of

feeling every vibration of pain and futility I could send, as, too, attested by her recognition of "Are you sincere?" as the deep-well sounded call from the bottom—"Baby, let's go home."

"We'll have to wait till Bromberg goes, take the train with him—I guess—." So I get up, go into the bathroom (where I'd been earlier while they were at the beach and sex-phantasized in remembrance of the time, on another even wilder and further back Bromberg weekend, poor Annie with her hair done up in curlers and her face no makeup and Leroy poor Leroy in the other room wondering what his wife's doing in there, and Leroy later driving off desperately into the night realizing we were up to something in the bathroom and so remembering myself now the pain I had caused Leroy that morning just for the sake of a little bit of sate for that worm and snake called sex)—I go into the bathroom and wash up and come down, trying to be cheerful.

Still I can't look at Mardou straight in the eye—in my heart, "O why did you do it?"—sensing, in my desperation, the prophecy of what's to come.

As if not enough this was the day of the night of the great Jones party, which was the night I jumped out of Mardou's cab and abandoned her to the dogs of war—the war man Yuri wages gainst man Leo, each one.—Beginning, Bromberg making phone-calls and gathering birthday gifts and getting ready to take the bus to make old 151 at 4:47 for the city, Sand driving us (a sorry lot indeed) to bus stop, where we have quick one in bar across street while Mardou by now ashamed not only of herself but me too stays in back seat of car (tho exhausted) but in broad daylight, trying to catch a wink—really trying to think her way out of trap only I could help her out of if I'm given one more chance—in the bar, parenthetically amazed I am to hear Bromberg going right on with big booming burbling comments on art and literature and even in fact by God queer anecdotes as sullen Santa Clara Valley farmers guzzle at rail, Bromberg doesn't even have consciousness of his fantastic impact on the ordinary—and Sand enjoying, himself in fact also weird—but minor details.—I come out to tell Mardou we have decided to take later train in order to go back to house to pick up forgotten package which is just another ringaroundtherosy of futility for her, she receives this news with solemn lips—ah my love and lost darling (out of date word)—if then I'd known what I know now, instead of returning to bar, for further talks, and looking at her with hurt eyes, etc., and let her lay there in the bleak sea of time untended and unsolaced and unforgiven for the sin of the sea of time I'd have gone in and sat down with her, taken her hand, promised her my life and protection—"Because I love you and there's no reason"—but then far from having completely successfully realized this love, I was still in the act of thinking I was climbing out of my doubt about her—but the train came, finally, 153 at 5:31 after all our delays, we got in, and rode to the city—through South San Francisco and past my house, facing one another in coach seats, riding by the big yards in Bayshore and I gleefully (trying to be gleeful) point out a kicked boxcar ramming a hopper and you see the tinscrap shuddering far off, wow—but most of the time sitting bleakly under either stare and saying, finally, "I really do feel I must be getting a rummy nose"—anything I could think of saying to ease the pressure of what I really wanted to weep about—but in the main the three of us really sad, riding together on a train to gayety, horror, the eventual H bomb.

—Bidding Austin adieu finally at some teeming corner on Market where Mardou and I wandered among great sad sullen crowds in a confusion mass, as if we were suddenly lost in the actual physical manifestation of the mental condition we'd been in now together for two months, not even holding hands but I anxiously leading the way through crowds (so's to get out fast, hated it) but really because I was too "hurt" to hold her hand

and remembering (now with greater pain) her usual insistence that I not hold her in the street or people'll think she's a hustler —ending up, in bright lost sad afternoon, down Price Street (O fated Price Street) towards Heavenly Lane, among the children, the young good-looking Mex chicks each one making me say to myself with contempt "Ah they're almost all of 'em better than Mardou, all I gotta do is get one of them . . . but O, but O"—neither one of us speaking much, and such chagrin in her eyes that in the original place where I had seen that Indian warmth which had originally prompted me to say to her, on some happy candlelit night, "Honey what I see in your eyes is a lifetime of affection not only from the Indian in you but because as part Negro somehow you are the first, the essential woman, and therefore the most, most originally most fully affectionate and maternal"—there now is the chagrin too, some lost American addition and mood with it—"Eden's in Africa," I'd added one time—but now in my hurt hate turning the other way and so walking down Price with her every time I see a Mexican gal or Negress I say to myself, "hustlers," they're all the same, always trying to cheat and rob you—harking back to all relations in the past with them—Mardou sensing these waves of hostility from me and silent.

And who's in our bed in Heavenly Lane but Yuri—cheerful —"Hey I been workin' all day, so tired I had to come back and get some more rest."—I decide to tell him everything, try to form the words in my mouth, Yuri sees my eyes, senses the tenseness, Mardou senses the tenseness, a knock on the door brings in John Golz (always romantically interested in Mardou in a naiver way), he senses the tenseness, "I've come to borrow a book"—grim expression on his face and remembering how I'd put him down about selectivity—so leaves at once, with book, and Yuri in getting up from bed (while Mardou hides behind screen to change from party dress to home jeans)—"Leo hand me my pants."—"Get up and get 'em yourself, they're right there on the chair, she can't see you"—a funny statement, and my mind feels funny and I look at Mardou who is silent and inward.

The moment she goes to the bathroom I say to Yuri "I'm very jealous about you and Mardou in the backseat last night man, I really am."—"It's not my fault, it was her started it." —"Lissen, you're such—like don't let her, keep away—you're such a lady-killer they all fall for you"—saying this just as Mardou returns, looking up sharply not hearing the words but seeing them in the air, and Yuri at once grabs the still open door and says "Well anyway I'm going to Adam's I'll see you there later."

"What did you tell Yuri—?" —I tell her word for word— "God the tenseness in here was unbearable"—(sheepishly I review the fact that instead of being stern and Moses-like in my jealousy and position I'd instead chatted with nervous "poet" talk with Yuri, as always, giving him the tension but not the positiveness of my feelings in words—sheepishly I review my sheepishness—I get sad to see old Carmody somehow—

"Baby I'm gonna—you think they got chickens on Columbus? —I've seen some—And cook it, see, we'll have a nice chicken supper."—"And," I say to myself, "what good is a nice domestic chicken supper when you love Yuri so much he has to leave the moment you walk in because of the pressure of my jealousy and your possibility as prophesied in a dream?" "I want" (out loud) "to see Carmody, I'm sad—you stay here, cook the chicken, eat—alone—I'll come back later and get you."—"But it always starts off like this, we always go away, we never stay alone." —"I know but tonight I'm sad I gotta see Carmody, for some reason don't ask me I have a tremendous sad desire and reason just to—after all I drew his picture the other day" (I had drawn my first pencil sketches of human figures reclining and they were greeted with amazement by Carmody and Adam and so I was proud) "and after all in drawing those shots of Frank

95

the other day I saw such great sadness in the lines under his eyes that I know he—" (to myself: I know he'll understand how sad I am now, I know he has suffered on four continents this way).—Pondering Mardou does not know which way to turn but suddenly I tell her of my quick talk with Yuri the part I'd forgotten in the first report (and here too) "He said to me 'Leo I don't want to make your girl Mardou, after all I have no eyes—'." "Oh, so he has no eyes! A hell of a thing to say!" (the same teeth of glee now the portals where pass angry winds, and her eyes glitter) and I hear that junkey-like emphasis on the *ings* where she presses down on her *ings* like many junkies I know, from some inside heavy somnolent reason, which in Mardou I'd attributed to her amazing modernness culled (as I once asked her) "From where? where did you learn all you know and that amazing way you speak?" but now to hear that interesting *ing* only makes me mad as it's coming in a transparent speech about Yuri where she shows she's not really against seeing Yuri again at party or otherwise, "if he's gonna talk like that about no eyes," she's gonna tell him.—"O," I say, "now you WANT to come to the party at Adam's, because there you can get even with Yuri and tell him off—you're so transparent."

"Jesus," as we're walking along the benches of the church park sad park of the whole summer season, "now you're calling me names, transparent."

"Well that's what it is, you think I can't see through that, at first you didn't want to go to Adam's at all and now that you hear—well the hell with that if it ain't transparent I don't know what is."—"Calling me names, Jesus" (shnuffling to laugh) and both of us actually hysterically smiling and as tho nothing had happened at all and in fact like happy unconcerned people you see in newsreels busy going down the street to their chores and where-go's and we're in the same rainy newsreel mystery sad but inside of us (as must then be so inside the puppet filmdolls of screen) the great tumescent turbulent turmoil alliterative as

96

a hammer on the brain bone bag and balls, bang I'm sorry I
was ever born. . . .

To cap everything, as if it wasn't enough, the whole world
opens up as Adam opens the door bowing solemnly but with a
glint and secret in his eye and some kind of unwelcomeness I
bristle at the sight of—"What's the matter?" Then I sense the
presence of more people in there than Frank and Adam and
Yuri.—"We have visitors."—"Oh," I say, "distinguished visitors?"—"I think so."—"Who?"—"Mac Jones and Phyllis."—
"What?" (the great moment has come when I'm to come face
to face, or leave, with my arch literary enemy Balliol Mac-
Jones erstwhile so close to me we used to slop beer on each
other's knees in leaning-over talk excitement, we'd talked and
exchanged and borrowed and read books and literarized so
much the poor innocent had actually come under some kind of
influence from me, that is, in the sense, only, that he learned the
talk and style, mainly the history of the hip or beat generation
or subterranean generation and I'd told him "Mac, write a great
book about everything that happened when Leroy came to New
York in 1949 and don't leave a word out and blow, go!" which
he did, and I read it, critically Adam and I in visits to his place
both critical of the manuscript but when it came out they guaran-
tee him 20,000 dollars an unheard of sum and all of us beat
types wandering the Beach and Market Street and Times Square
when in New York, tho Adam and I had solemnly admitted, quote,
"Jones is not of us—but from another world—the midtown
sillies world" (an Adamism). And so his great success coming
at the moment when I was poorest and most neglected by publishers and worse than that hung-up on paranoiac drug habits I
became incensed but I didn't get too mad, but stayed black
about it, changing my mind after father time's few local scythes
and various misfortunes and trips around, writing him apolo-
getic letters on ships which I tore up, he too writing them mean-
while, and then, Adam acting a year later as some kind of saint

97

and mediator reported favorable inclinations on both our parts, to both parties—the great moment when I would have to face old Mac and shake with him and call it quits, let go all the rancor—making as little impression on Mardou, who is so independent and unavailable in that new heartbreaking way. Anyway MacJones was there, immediately I said out loud "Good, great, I been wantin' to see him," and I rushed into the living-room and over someone's head who was getting up (Yuri it was) I shook hands firmly with Balliol, sat brooding awhile, didn't even notice how poor Mardou had managed to position herself (here as at Bromberg's as everywhere poor dark angel) —finally going to the bedroom unable to bear the polite conversation under which not only Yuri but Jones (and also Phyllis his woman who kept staring at me to see if it was still crazy) rumbled, I ran to the bedroom and lay in the dark and at the first opportunity tried to get Mardou to lie down with me but she said "Leo I don't want to lay around in here in the dark." —Yuri then coming over, putting on one of Adam's ties, saying, "I'm going out and find me a girl," and we have a kind of whispering rapport now away from them in the parlor—all's forgiven.—But I feel that because Jones does not move from his couch he really doesn't want to talk to me and probably wishes secretly I'd leave, when Mardou roams back again to my bed of shame and sorrow and hidingplace, I say, "What are you talking about in there, bop? Don't tell *him* anything about music."—(Let him find out for himself! I say to myself pettishly)—*I'm* the bop writer!—But as I'm commissioned to get the beer downstairs, when I come in again with beer in arms they're all in the kitchen, Mac foremost, smiling, and saying, "Leo! let me see those drawings they told me you did, I want to see them."—So we become friends again bending over drawings and Yuri has to be showing his too (he draws) and Mardou is in the other room, again forgotten—but it is a historic moment and as we also, with Carmody, study Carmody's South American

bleak pictures of high jungle villages and Andean towns where
you can see the clouds pass, I notice Mac's expensive good-
looking clothes, wrist watch, I feel proud of him and now he has
an attractive little mustache that makes his maturity—which I
announce to everyone—the beer by now warming us all up, and
then his wife Phyllis begins a supper and the conviviality flows
back and forth—

In the red bulblight parlor in fact I see Jones alone with
Mardou questioning, as if interviewing her, I see that he's grin-
ning and saying to himself 'Old Percepied's got himself another
amazing doll' and I inside yearn to myself, "Yeah, for how
long"—and he's listening to Mardou, who, impressed, forewarned,
understanding everything, makes solemn statements about bop,
like, "I don't like bop, I really don't, it's like junk to me, too
many junkies are bop men and I hear the junk in it."—"Well,"
Mac adjusting glasses, "that's interesting."—And I go up and
say, "But you never like what you come from" (looking at Mardou).—"What do you mean?"—"You're the child of Bop," or
the children of bop, some such statement, which Mac and I
agree on—so that later when we all the whole gang troop out to
further festivities of the night, and Mardou, wearing Adam's
long black velvet jacket (for her long) and a mad long scarf
too, looking like a little Polish underground girl or boy in a
sewer beneath the city and cute and hip, and in the street rushes
up from one group to the one I'm in, and I reach out as she
reaches me (I'm wearing Carmody's felt hat straight on my head
like hipster for joke and my red shirt still, now defunct from
weekends) and sweep her littleness off her feet and up against
me and go on walking carrying her, I hear Mac's appreciative
"Wow" and "Go" laugh in the background and I think proudly
"He sees now that I have a real great chick—that I am not dead
but going on—old continuous Percepied—never getting older,
always in there, always with the young, the new generations—."
A motley group in any case going down the street what with

Adam Moorad wearing a full tuxedo borrowed from Sam the night before so he could attend some opening with tickets free from his office—trooping down to Dante's and Mask again—that Mask, that old po mask all the time—Dante's where in the rise and roar of the social and gab excitement I looked up many times to catch Mardou's eyes and play eyes with her but she seemed reluctant, abstract, brooding—no longer affectionate of me—sick of all our talk, with Bromberg re-arriving and great further discourses and that particular noxious group-enthusiasm that you're supposed to feel when like Mardou you're with a star of the group or even I mean just a member of that constellation, how noisome, tiresome it must have been to her to have to appreciate all we were saying, to be amazed by the latest quip from the lips of the one and only, the newest manifestation of the same old dreary mystery of personality in KaJa the great —disgusted she seemed indeed, and looking into space.

So later when in my drunkenness I managed to get Paddy Cordavan over to our table and he invited us all to his place for further drinking (the usually unattainable social Paddy Cordavan due to his woman who always wanted to go home alone with him, Paddy Cordavan of whom Buddy Pond had said, "He's too beautiful I can't look," tall, blond, big-jawed somber Montana cowboy slowmoving, slow talking, slow shouldered) Mardou wasn't impressed, as she wanted to get away from Paddy and all the other subterraneans of Dante's anyway, whom I had just freshly annoyed by yelling again at Julien, "Come here, we're all going to Paddy's party and Julien's coming," at which Julien immediately leaped up and rushed back to Ross Wallenstein and the others at their own booth, thinking, "God that awful Percepied is screaming at me and trying to drag me to his silly places again, I wish someone would do something about him." And Mardou wasn't any further impressed when, at Yuri's insistence, I went to the phone and spoke to Sam (calling from work) and agreed to meet him later at the bar across from the

office—"We'll all go! we'll all go!" I'm screaming by now and
even Adam and Frank are yawning ready to go home and Jones
is long gone—rushing around up and down Paddy's stairs for
further calls with Sam and at one point here I am rushing into
Paddy's kitchen to get Mardou to come meet Sam with me and
Ross Wallenstein having arrived while I was in the bar calling
says, looking up, "Who let this guy in, hey, who is this? how'd
you get in here! Hey Paddy!" in serious continuation of his
original dislike and "are-you-a-fag" come-on, which I ignored,
saying, "Brother I'll take the fuzz off your peach if you don't
shut up," or some such putdown, can't remember, strong enough
to make him swivel like a soldier, the way he does, stiff necked,
and retire—I dragging Mardou down to a cab to rush to Sam's
and all this wild world swirling night and she in her little voice
I hear protesting from far away, "But Leo, dear Leo, I want to
go home and sleep."—"Ah hell!" and I give Sam's address to
the taxidriver, she says NO, insists, gives Heavenly Lane, "Take
me there first and then go to Sam's" but I'm really seriously
hung-up on the undeniable fact that if I take her to Heavenly
Lane first the cab will never make it to Sam's waiting bar before
closing time, so I argue, we harangue hurling different addresses
at the cab driver who like in a movie waits, but suddenly, with
that red flame that same red flame (for want of a better image)
I leap out of the cab and rush out and there's another one, I
jump in, give Sam's address and off he guns her—Mardou left
in the night, in a cab, sick, and tired, and me intending to pay
the second cab with the buck she'd entrusted to Adam to get
her a sandwich but which in the turmoil had been forgotten but
he gave it to me for her—poor Mardou going home alone, again,
and drunken maniac was gone.

Well, I thought, this is the end—I finally made the step and
by God I paid her back for what she done to me—it had to
come and this is it—ploop.

101

Isn't it good to know winter is coming—
and that life will be a little
more quiet—and you will be home
writing and eating well and we will
be spending pleasant nights wrapped
round one another—and you are home
now, rested and eating well because you
should not become too sad—and I feel
better when I know you are well.

and

Write to me   Anything.
Please stay well
Your Freind
And my love
And Oh
And Love for You
MARDOU
Please

BUT THE DEEPEST premonition and prophesy of all had always been, that when I walked into Heavenly Lane, cutting in sharply from sidewalk, I'd look up, and if Mardou's light was on Mardou's light was on—"But some day, dear Leo, that light will not shine for you"—this a prophesy irrespective of all your Yuris and attenuations in the snake of time.—"Someday she won't be there when you want her to be there, the light'll be out and you'll be looking up and it will be dark in Heavenly Lane and Mardou'll be gone, and it'll be when you least expect it and want it."—Always I knew this—it crossed my mind that night when I ran up, met Sam in the bar, he was with two newspapermen, we bought drinks, I spilled money on the floor, I hurried to get drunk (through with my baby!), rushed up to Adam and Frank's, woke them up again, wrestled on the floor, made noise, Sam tore my T-shirt off, bashed the lamp in, drank a fifth of bourbon as of old in our tremendous days together, it was just another big downcrashing in the night and all for nothing . . . waking up, I, in the morning with the final hangover that said to me, "Too late"—and got up and staggered to the door through the debris, and opened it, and went home, Adam saying to me as he heard me fiddle with the groaning faucet, "Leo go home and recuperate well," sensing how sick I was tho not knowing about Mardou and me—and at home I wandered around, couldn't stay in the house, couldn't stop, had to walk, as if someone was going to die soon, as if I could smell the flowers of death in the air, and I went in the South San Francisco railyard and cried.

Cried in the railyard sitting on an old piece of iron under the new moon and on the side of the old Southern Pacific tracks, cried because not only I had cast off Mardou whom now I was not so sure I wanted to cast off but the die'd been thrown, feeling too her empathetic tears across the night and the final horror both of us round-eyed realizing we part—but seeing suddenly not in the face of the moon but somewhere in the sky as I looked up and hoped to figure, the face of my mother—remembering it in fact from a haunted nap just after supper that same restless unable-to-stay-in-a-chair or on-earth day—just as I woke to some Arthur Godfrey program on the TV, I saw bending over me the visage of my mother, with impenetrable eyes and moveless lips and round cheekbones and glasses that glinted and hid the major part of her expression which at first I thought was a vision of horror that I might shudder at, but it didn't make me shudder —wondering about it on the walk and suddenly now in the railyards weeping for my lost Mardou and so stupidly because I'd decided to throw her away myself, it had been a vision of my mother's love for me—that expressionless and expressionless-because-so-profound face bending over me in the vision of my sleep, and with lips not so pressed together as enduring and as if to say, *"Pauvre Ti Leo, pauvre Ti Leo, tu souffri, les hommes*

103

souffri tant, y'ainque toi dans le monde j'va't prendre soin,
j'aim'ra beaucoup t'prendre soin tous tes jours mon ange."—
"Poor Little Leo, poor Little Leo, you suffer, men suffer so,
you're all alone in the world I'll take care of you, I would very
much like to take care of you all your days my angel."—My
mother an angel too—the tears welled up in my eyes, something
broke, I cracked—I had been sitting for an hour, in front of me
was Butler Road and the gigantic rose neon ten blocks long
BETHLEHEM WEST COAST STEEL with stars above and the
smashby Zipper and the fragrance of locomotive coalsmoke as I
sit there and let them pass and far down the line in the night
around that South San Francisco airport you can see that sonofabitch red light waving Mars signal light swimming in the dark
big red markers blowing up and down and sending fires in the
keenpure lostpurity lovelyskies of old California in the late sad
night of autumn spring comefall winter's summertime tall, like
trees—the only man in South City who ever walked from the
neat suburban homes and went and hid by boxcars to think—
broke.—Something fell loose in me—O blood of my soul I
thought and the Good Lord or whatever's put me here to suffer
and groan and on top of that be guilty and gives me the flesh
and blood that is so painful the—women all mean well—this
I knew—women love, bend over you—you'd as soon betray a
woman's love as spit on your own feet, clay—

That sudden short crying in the railyard and for a reason I
really didn't fathom, and couldn't—saying to myself in the
bottom, "You see a vision of the face of the woman who is your
mother who loves you so much she has supported you and pro-
tected you for years, you a bum, a drunkard—never complained
a jot—because she knows that in your present state you can't
go out in the world and make a living and take care of yourself
and even find and hold the love of another protecting woman—
and all because you are poor stupid Ti Leo—deep in the dark
pit of night under the stars of the world you are lost, poor, no

104

one cares, and now you threw away a little woman's love because you wanted another drink with a rowdy fiend from the other side of your insanity."

And as always.

Ending with the great sorrow of Price Street when Mardou and I, reunited on Sunday night according to my schedule (I'd made up the schedule that week thinking in a yard tea-reverie, "This is the cleverest arrangement I ever made, why with this thing I can live a full love-life," conscious of Mardou's Reichian worth, and at the same time write those three novels and be a big—etc.) (schedule all written out, and delivered to Mardou for her perusal, it said, "Go to Mardou at 9 in the evening, sleep, return following noon for afternoon of writing and evening supper and aftersupper rest and then return at 9 P.M. again," with holes in the schedule left open on weekends for "possible going out") (getting plastered)—with this schedule still in mind and after spending the weekend at home steeped in that awful —I rushed anyway to Mardou's on Sunday night at 9 P.M., as scheduled, there was no light in her window ("Just as I knew it would happen someday")—but on the door a note, and for me, which I read after quick leak in the hall john—"Dear Leo, I'll be back at 10:30," and the door (as always) unlocked and I go in to wait and read Reich—carrying again my big forward-looking healthybook Reich and ready at least to "throw a good one in her" in case it's all bound to end this very night and sitting there eyes shifting around and plotting—11:30 and she hasn't come yet—fearing me—missing—("Leo," later, she told me, "I really thought we were through, that you wouldn't come back at all")—nevertheless she'd left that Bird of Paradise note for me, always and still hoping and not aiming to hurt me and keep me waiting in dark—but because she does not return at 11:30 I cut out, to Adam's, leaving message for her to call, with ramifications that I erase after a while—all a host of minor details leading to the great sorrow of Price Street taking place after we spend a night of "successful" sex, when I tell her, "Mardou you've become much more precious to me since everything that happened," and because of that, as we agree, I am able to make her fulfill better, which she does—twice, in fact, and for the first time—spending a whole sweet afternoon as if reunited but at intervals poor Mardou looking up and saying, "But we should really break up, we've never done anything together, we were going to Mexico, and then you were going to get a job and we'd live together, then remember the loft idea, all big phantasm that like haven't worked out because you haven't pushed them from your mind out into the open world, haven't acted on them, and like, me, I don't—I've missed my therapist for weeks." (She'd written a fine letter that very day to the therapist begging forgiveness and permission to come back in a few weeks and advice for her lostness and I'd approved of it.)—All of this unreal from the moment I walked into Heavenly Lane after my crying-in-the-railyard lonely dark sojourn at home to see her light was out at last (as deeply promised), but the note, saving us awhile, my finding her a little later that night as she did finally call me at Adam's and told me to come to Rita's, where I brought beer, then Mike Murphy came and he brought beer too—ending with another silly yelling conversation drunk night.—Mardou saying in the morning, "Do you remember anything you said last night to Mike and Rita?" and me, "Of course not."—The whole day, borrowed from the sky day, sweet—we make love and try to make promises of little kinds—no go, as in the evening she says "Let's go to a show" (with her pitiful check money).—"Jesus, we'll spend all your money."—"Well goddamit I don't care, I'm going to spend that money and that's all there is to it," with great emphasis—so she puts on her black velvet slacks and some perfume and I go up and smell her neck and God, how sweet can you smell—and I want her more than ever, in my arms she's gone—in my hand she's as slippy as dust—something's wrong.—"Did I cut you when I jumped out of the cab?"—"Leo, it was baby, it was the most maniacal thing I ever saw."—"I'm sorry."—"I know you're sorry but it was the most maniacal thing I ever *saw* and it keeps happening and getting worse and like, now, oh hell—let's go to a show."—So we go out, and she has on this little heartbreaking never-seen-by-me before red raincoat over the black velvet slacks and cuts along, with black short hair making her look so strange, like a —like someone in Paris—I have on just my old ex-brakeman railroad Cant Bust Ems and a workshirt without undershirt and suddenly it's cold October out there, and with gusts of rain, so I shiver at her side as we hurry up Price Street—towards Market, shows—I remember that afternoon returning from the Bromberg weekend—something is caught in both our throats, I don't know what, she does.

"Baby I'm going to tell you something and if I tell it to you I want you to promise nevertheless you'll come to the movie with me."—"Okay."—And naturally I add, after pause, "What is it?"—I think it has something to do with "Let's break up really and truly, I don't want to make it, not because I don't like you but it's by now or should be obvious to both of us by now—" that kind of argument that I can, as of yore and again, break, by saying, "But let's, look, I have, wait—" for always the man can make the little woman bend, she was made to bend, the little woman was—so I wait confidently for this kind of talk, tho feel bleak, tragic, grim, and the air cold.—"You know the other night" (she spends some time trying to order confused nights of recent—and I help her straighten them out, and have my arm around her waist, as we cut along we come closer to the brittle jewel lights of Price and Columbus that old North Beach corner so weird and ever weirder now and I have my private thoughts about it as from older scenes in my San Francisco life, in brief, almost smug and snug in the rug of myself —in any case we agree that the night she means to tell me about is Saturday night, which was the night I cried in the railyards

107

—that short sudden, as I say, crying, that vision—I'm trying
in fact to interpose and tell her about it, trying also to figure
out if she means now that on Saturday night something awful
happened that I should know—).

"Well I went to Dante's and didn't want to stay, and tried to
leave—and Yuri was trying to hang around—and he called
somebody—and I was at the phone—and told Yuri he was
wanted" (as incoherent as that) "and while he is in the booth
I cut on home, because I was tired—baby at two o'clock in the
morning he came and knocked on the door—"

"Why?"—"For a place to sleep, he was drunk, he rushed in
—and—well—."

"Huh?"

"Well baby we made it together,"—that hip word—at the
sound of which even as I walked and my legs propelled under
me and my feet felt firm, the lower part of my stomach sagged
into my pants or loins and the body experienced a sensation of
deep melting downgoing into some soft somewhere, nowhere—
suddenly the streets were so bleak, the people passing so beastly,
the lights so unnecessary just to illumine this . . . this cutting
world—it was going across the cobbles when she said it, "made
it together," I had (locomotive wise) to concentrate on getting
up on the curb again and I didn't look at her—I looked down
Columbus and thought of walking away, rapidly, as I'd done at
Larry's—I didn't—I said "I don't want to live in this beastly
world"—but so low she barely if at all heard me and if so never
commented, but after a pause she added a few things, like,
"There are other details, like, what—but I won't go into them
—like," stammering, and slow—yet both of us swinging along
in the street to the show—the show being *Brave Bulls* (I cried
to see the grief in the matador when he heard his best friend
and girl had gone off the mountain in his own car, I cried to
see even the bull that I knew would die and I knew the big deaths
bulls do die in their trap called bullring)—I wanted to run away

108

from Mardou. ("Look man," she'd said only a week before when I'd suddenly started talking about Adam and Eve and referred to her as Eve, the woman who by her beauty is able to make the man do anything, "don't call me Eve.")—But now no matter —walking along, at one point so irritable to my senses she stopped short on the rainy sidewalk and coolly said "I need a neckerchief" and turned to go into the store and I turned and followed her from reluctant ten feet back realizing I hadn't known what was going on in my mind really ever since Price and Columbus and here we were on Market—while she's in the store I keep haggling with myself, shall I just go now, I have my fare, just cut down the street swiftly and go home and when she comes out she'll see you're gone, she'll know you broke the promise to go to the movies just like you broke a lot of promises but this time she'll know you have a big male right to—but none of this is enough—I feel stabbed by Yuri—by Mardou I feel forsaken and shamed—I turn to look in the store blindly at anything and there she comes at just that moment wearing a phosphorescent purple bandana (because big raindrops had just started flying and she didn't want the rain to string out her carefully combed for the movies hair and here she was spending her small monies on kerchiefs.)—In the movie I hold her hand, after a fifteen-minute wait, not thinking to at all not because I was mad but I felt she would feel it was too subservient at this time to take her hand in the movieshow, like lovers—but I took her hand, she was warm, lost—ask not the sea why the eyes of the dark-eyed woman are strange and lost—came out of the movie, I glum, she businesslike to get through the cold to the bus, where, at the bus stop, she walked away from me to lead me to a warmer waiting place and (as I said) I'd mentally accused her of wanderingfoot.

Arriving home, where we sat, she on my lap, after a long warm talk with John Golz, who came in to see her, but found me too, and might have left, but in my new spirit I wanted at once to show him that I respected and liked him, and talked with him, and he stayed two hours—in fact I saw how he annoyed Mardou by talking literature with her beyond the point where she was interested and also about things she'd long known about—poor Mardou.

So he left, and I curled her on my lap, and she talked about the war between men—"They have a war, to them a woman is a prize, to Yuri it's just that your prize has less value now."

"Yeah," I say, sad, "but I should have paid more attention to the old junkey nevertheless, who said there's a lover on every corner—they're all the same, boy, don't get hung-up on one."

"It isn't true, it isn't true, that's just what Yuri wants is for you to go down to Dante's now and the two of you'll laugh and talk me over and agree that women are good lays and there are a lot of them.—I think you're like me—you want one love— like, men have the essence in the woman, there's an essence" ("Yes," I thought, "there's an essence, and that is your womb") "and the man has it in his hand, but rushes off to build big constructions." (I'd just read her the first few pages of *Finnegans Wake* and explained them and where Finnegan is always putting up "buildung supra buildung supra buildung" on the banks of the Liffey—dung!)

"I will say nothing," I thought—"Will you think I am not a man if I don't get mad?"

"Just like that war I told you about."

"Women have wars too—"

Oh what'll we do? I think—now I go home, and it's all over for sure, not only now is she bored and has had enough but has pierced me with an adultery of a kind, has been inconstant, as prophesied in a dream, the dream the bloody dream—I see myself grabbing Yuri by the shirt and throwing him on the floor, he pulls out a Yugoslavian knife, I pick up a chair to bash him with, everybody's watching . . . but I continue the daydream and I look into his eyes and I see suddenly the glare of a jester

110

angel who made his presence on earth all a joke and I realize that this too with Mardou was a joke and I think, "Funny Angel, elevated amongst the subterraneans."

"Baby it's up to you," is what she's actually saying, "about how many times you wanta see me and all that—but I want to be independent like I say."

And I go home having lost her love.

And write this book.

CPSIA information can be obtained
at www.ICGtesting.com
Printed in the USA
JSHW041302271121
20813JS00005B/5

9 780802 131867